PENGUIN BOOKS

THE GIRL WHO KNEW TOO MUCH

Vikrant Khanna is a captain in the Merchant Navy. He is the bestselling author of *Secretly Yours*, *When Life Tricked Me* and *Love Lasts Forever*. Apart from writing, he is fond of composing songs and playing the guitar. He lives in New Delhi.

He can be contacted here:
Facebook: www.facebook.com/writervikrant/
Twitter: www.twitter.com/_VikrantKhanna
Instagram: www.instagram.com/vikrantkhanna/

Secretly Yours

VIKRANT KHANNA

THE GIRL WHO KNEW TOO MUCH

What if the loved one you lost were to come back?

EBURY
PRESS

An imprint of Penguin Random House

EBURY PRESS

USA | Canada | UK | Ireland | Australia
New Zealand | India | South Africa | China

Ebury Press is part of the Penguin Random House group of companies
whose addresses can be found at global.penguinrandomhouse.com

Published by Penguin Random House India Pvt. Ltd
4th Floor, Capital Tower 1, MG Road,
Gurugram 122 002, Haryana, India

Penguin
Random House
India

First published in Penguin Books by Penguin Random House India 2017

This edition published in Ebury Press by Penguin Random House India 2020

29 28 27 26 25

ISBN 9780143439943

Typeset in Adobe Garamond Pro by Manipal Digital Systems, Manipal
Printed at Replika Press Pvt. Ltd, India

www.penguin.co.in

MIX
Paper from
responsible sources
FSC® C016779

To my grandmother, for instilling faith in me

Before you begin reading the book, take a moment to decide:

Are you a believer or a cynic?

One

It isn't often that you see a little girl, all by herself, crouched on a bench in a remote corner of a park.

I looked around. The park was moderately occupied for a Saturday evening—kids screaming with joy on colourful swings; oldies holding their walking sticks and padding slowly on the zigzag tracks; young couples hiding behind bushes, landing watchful kisses on each other—and yet, no one seemed to notice this girl.

She would be no more than twelve, or thirteen perhaps. She had her legs drawn up to her chest and her head rested on her knees. Her long hair shrouded her face almost in entirety.

As I approached her, I realized she was crying. A knot tightened in my chest. I took a seat next to her. Her curved back moved up and down as she sobbed. Her right hand flew to her nose, wiping it, and at that moment, her face tilted a little to my side. She grew conscious of my presence and shifted her head to the other side, ceasing her sobs for the time being.

From the little that I saw of her face, she came across as a pretty child, hailing from an affluent family. Her dark blue jeans, with the Zara tag sticking out, bright pink T-shirt and a pair of brand new magenta Crocs confirmed my assessment.

Carefully, she turned her head and still finding me there, jerked it back to the other side. I smiled.

'It's okay,' I said. 'You can cry.'

She remained quiet.

'Crying is good,' I said, craning my neck to catch a glimpse of her face. 'It helps dissolve some of the pain.'

She said nothing but shook her head vigorously, her long and soft hair swaying all over.

I figured she was crying because her father probably refused to give her a toy or something. I knew these rich kids; they could never be happy. We had plenty of spoilt kids like her in this neighbourhood of south Delhi, who wanted nothing less than heaven on Earth.

In the western part of the sky, the sun shone brightly. It would take more than an hour for dusk to arrive.

Although her sobs had ceased, the kid's posture remained unchanged: legs up to her chest, arms wrapped around her knees and face turned to the other side.

'Are you okay now?'

She lifted her head, ran a clumsy hand across it and for the first time, turned to me, nodding just a little. She looked like one of those cute kids from the advertisements on TV. She had a perfectly round face, big eyes and exceptionally flawless skin. Her eyes were soggy and the skin below it wrinkled. She curled her lips and another bout of tears emerged.

'Why are you so sad? What happened? Tell me, I'll help you.'

She shook her head again. 'You can't help me. No one can.'

'Try me,' I said.

She gave a loud sniff and wiped her eyes. Now my heart went out to her. It is heartbreaking to watch kids cry.

'Okay, let me guess,' I said, moving closer to her. 'Your father didn't get you a . . . a . . . Barbie doll?'

She frowned, wrinkling her nose and narrowing her eyes to slits. 'I'm not a kid! I don't cry for such foolish reasons!'

I frowned. 'Not a kid? How old are you?'

'Thirteen.'

'So well, you are a kid.'

She shrugged and looked ahead. I smiled and shook my head. Perhaps, calling a kid a kid is not a cool thing. But at least this conversation managed to disrupt her sobs.

'Oh, by the way, I didn't even ask your name.'

She looked at me, her head tilting just a bit as though in pride. 'Akshara Malhotra.'

'And my name is Harvinder,' I said. 'But you can call me Harry.'

'Why should I call you Harry if your name is Harvinder?'

I sputtered a quick laugh. 'Because that's my nickname. I like it. Don't you have a nickname?'

'No.'

'Actually, you don't need one. You have a pretty name.'

Her face glistened, a flush rising up her cheeks. 'My mother gave it to me.' And the flush disappeared as quickly as it came. Tears welled up in her eyes again.

My heart thudded in my chest as the sudden realization hit me.

She nodded, slowly choking on her sobs. 'She . . . she died.'

Two

I couldn't get Akshara to stop weeping. Her little palms kneaded her eyes as if to stop the tears from running out. They couldn't. I asked her how long it had been since her mother died. With difficulty, she answered: 'Two weeks.'

My heart sank. 'I'm so, so sorry, baby.'

It's not that I haven't seen people cry or heard stories of death, but I feel the most distressing separation is that of a mother and her daughter.

'You know, Harry, I read a few days ago in one of Mummy's old books that . . . that . . .' She swallowed hard. 'When you . . . when you always remember a loved one who has died, miss them, cry for them, they become your guardian angel and are always with you. It was so . . .' She couldn't complete her statement as a fit of sobs choked her.

'Oh, Akshara, please, please don't cry, baby. Everything's going to be all right.'

She made the kind of pitiable face only a kid can make, rolling her lower lip over the upper, eliciting copious amounts of pity. 'Mummy died. How can everything be all right?'

'You have your father, right? Where's he?'

She looked to her left. Along the periphery of the park, a neat jogging track went as far as the eyes could reach. 'He's not here,' she said, looking back at me. 'He's hardly here.'

'What do you mean?'

'He's always travelling. He's nice but he's hardly home.'

'So who do you stay with?'

'Shilpi Aunty.'

'Who's Shilpi Aunty?'

'She's our maid . . .' She clucked her tongue. 'No, no, she's my aunty.' Then she narrowed her eyes and with a tiny sense of regret said, 'Mummy never liked it if I called her that.'

Few moments later, she told me her father was good but her mother was the best.

'You know, Harry, don't you?' she asked, peering up at me through her teary eyes. 'That a man cannot love as deeply as a woman?'

I was startled. It was the second time during this conversation that I felt this kid was smarter for her age. I felt an overpowering urge to hug her and wish all her pain away, but I couldn't do that. When she grew inconsolable, I decided to tell her a story that might just help her.

'What kind of story?' she asked, a little interested already.

'A story of miracles,' I replied. 'Well, do you know what a miracle is?'

'Of course I know, Harry. When something happens through a supernatural intervention, it's a miracle.'

I raised my eyebrows in admiration. 'Bingo, girl!'

She smiled and her eyes lit up.

'You like stories?'

'I love stories,' she replied with glee. 'I read books all the time. It's my favourite hobby.'

'Nice,' I said. 'So what kind of books do you read?'

Without even pondering over it, she said, excitedly, 'Fantasies!' Her eyes were the size of a football now. 'I love, love that world, Harry. Everything is possible in it.'

'Come to think of it, if you really try, everything is possible in this world as well.'

'No, Harry,' she said, shaking her head. 'I don't think so. Anyway, what's your story about?'

'It's your lucky day today, Akshara—it's a fantasy!'

Her hands flew to her mouth in disbelief. 'Really?' she asked, withdrawing them slowly.

'Really.'

'Is the story good?'

'Oh yes, very.'

She wiped her eyes with the back of her hands until they were dry. 'But why are you telling me this story?'

'Because this story will help you.'

'How?'

'You'll know by the end of it.'

She nodded with an air of uncertainty and said, 'Okay.'

'Now, I want you to listen to this story very carefully,' I said. 'It's the story of a girl named Sahiba, the love of her life and a little bit of magic.'

In a flash, Akshara corkscrewed her body towards me and sat cross-legged, her elbows on her knees and fists squeezing her cheeks.

I knew then that she was going to love the story.

Three

In 2004, when I first met Sahiba Sethi, I was sixteen years old and she was fourteen. I still remember the day vividly. The sun was shining brightly and there wasn't a single cloud in the sky. It was early September, my favourite month (Sahiba was born in September). Summer had worn off by then in Delhi and winter was a good two months away. Everything appeared greener and the scent in the air was dewy and intoxicating.

I was standing in the balcony of my first-floor apartment, staring down at the family shifting in to our neighbourhood. There she stood, along with her father—a short-statured, dark-complexioned man overseeing the transfer of furniture from the back of the truck to the apartment. Her mother, tall and fair, was busy talking on her phone, while her elder sister, good-looking even from a distance, was trying to gesture something to her.

Sahiba, in contrast to her, was not conventionally pretty. She was short and slightly plump, and as I would later notice, her hair was always oily and messy, and her cheeks full of pimples. But her eyes were beautiful: deep-set, big and expressive, adding to the charm and innocence of her face, which was in striking contrast to the shrewd and sharp features of her sister's.

Sahiba held the cutest dog in her arms—a golden retriever that would later grow into a giant. With one hand petting her dog, Sahiba surveyed the surroundings. Mine was a decent neighbourhood: four identical red-coloured buildings along the periphery of the compound, with a small park and a kids' play area in the centre. I lived in the outermost, right-hand building and Sahiba was moving in to the building to the left.

She spun around, glanced up and suddenly caught my gaze. I gave her an embarrassed smile of someone who was caught doing something he shouldn't have. She smiled back briefly and dropped her gaze, not lifting her eyes again.

Now, most people believe that love at first sight is a thing you only see in books or movies, but I can vouch for it: love at first sight is very much real. In fact, it is the best way to fall in love. You don't waste time being friends, getting to know the other person and so on. You straightaway get to the point of falling in love.

And on that bright, sunny Wednesday morning, I fell in love with Sahiba.

~

Over the next two years or so, I could never amass the courage to convey my feelings to her. We had a 'Oh, hey', 'hello' or 'bye' going on between us but we never had a real conversation. It did not worry me though, as she never interacted with boys. I always saw her with girls. She was in an all girls' school and she only had girlfriends. Her best friend, Ginny (I don't think that was her real name and till date, I don't know what it is), also from our neighbourhood, was like her—I never saw her with boys either. Perhaps that's why they got along so well.

Ginny was shorter than Sahiba, and those days I'd think that was why Sahiba mostly hung out with her—to feel taller. But that wasn't the case. They really were best friends. Whenever I'd eavesdrop on them, (by the way, I eavesdrop a lot; it's my favourite hobby), I'd hear them sharing . . . well, everything there was to share.

Like how in the summer of 2007, the day after her seventeenth birthday, Sahiba had seen the underwear of her PT instructor as he bent over to teach them a certain exercise in the school playground.

'What colour was it?' asked Ginny, with the seriousness of a patient asking a doctor for a diagnosis.

'Red,' replied Sahiba. 'My God, his trousers had such a big, gaping hole. And then he'd scream, "This is not how it's done! You people are not paying attention! I don't know where you are looking. Look at me, just look at what I'm doing." And then he'd bend over again. We never got that exercise right!'

The two girls burst out laughing.

'Which reminds me,' said Ginny, after a hearty laugh. 'I need to buy new underwear too. Mine are all so loose now; I fear they might just slip down my skirt.'

'Really?' exclaimed Sahiba with a grin. 'It became loose even for your tiny, little twenty-six inch waist?'

'Actually, it's twenty-four!'

'Ha!'

'And what's yours?'

'Thirty-two.'

'And I'm sure Siddharth teases you for it.'

'Sidhu, teasing me?' She rolled her eyes in disbelief. 'Never! He's the best.'

Oh wait, I didn't tell you about Siddharth aka Sidhu, did I? He was Sahiba's love interest, my arch nemesis.

See, I always thought there was plenty of time to tell Sahiba how I felt about her since she wasn't going anywhere and because of her apparent disinterest in boys. But later, I realized, in matters of the heart, one shouldn't wait.

Although, like I said earlier, she knew I existed and we'd acknowledge each other whenever we crossed paths, I don't think she had a clue about the amorous sighs I'd let out when I was around her. It was all because of her big, beautiful eyes. When she blinked and smiled at me, a light would flicker in the dark corners of my heart as if someone had flicked on a switch.

But when, one day, I saw her with a guy not too far from our neighbourhood near the old bus stop, I knew I had screwed up. They were holding hands and staring deep into each other's eyes. Sahiba didn't even notice me despite the gentle, deliberate grazing of our shoulders as I passed her.

I looked at the person who'd stolen my girl. He was at least a foot taller than Sahiba, thin, with a wisp of unkempt hair over his head and her exact pudgy nose. It was as good as a photocopy; only his was a little bigger and flattened out, as if a bulldozer had run over it. He was wearing loose blue denims and a tee that was equally huge for his thin chest. I don't know what Sahiba saw in him. Not that I had the looks of a Greek God. But at least I had a good, sharp nose.

That night I couldn't sleep and decided something had to be done about this guy.

I wasn't going to give up so easily on my first love.

Four

Now I understand I'm telling you this story a little bit out of sequence, but that's because all this happened a good eight to nine years ago. Although I remember exactly what happened in the end, I can't arrange the events chronologically. Therefore, I'm going to recount the events as and when I recall them.

I learnt much later how Sahiba met Siddharth. Of course, I got this information while eavesdropping on one of Sahiba's and Ginny's endless conversations in our park.

There were at least a dozen benches scattered along the park, but they would always sit on the one just beside the children's tiny play area. If that bench was occupied, they would walk along the periphery of the park until it was deserted. I always thought they preferred that bench so their talks could drown out in the clatter of the kids nearby, but unfortunately for them, their voices were so shrill and rang with such abundant excitement that anyone nearby could have just as easily heard them as me.

That day, the bench was vacant and just when the sun was about to set, they took their positions. If memory serves me right, this was some time in March 2007. I hovered behind them and listened to their conversation intently. Sahiba was telling Ginny that she was very fortunate to have met Siddharth.

'He's different,' she said. 'He really is. I can say that just by the way he looks at me.'

Ginny gave her a tiny smile as she flicked away her shoulder-length hair. Then, with a sudden curiosity and concern in equal measure, she asked, 'Has he recovered from the accident?'

'Oh yes, yes,' Sahiba said with a nod. 'Thank God. It's just a scar above his eye now.'

'And how much did you pray for him this time?' Ginny asked and thrust her hand into Sahiba's arm. 'Wait, wait, you don't need to answer that. I mean, you pray to God for a couple of hours for a stupid exam. So I can imagine how much you must have prayed for his recovery.'

'Four hours every day for two months,' Sahiba replied nevertheless.

'My God,' said Ginny, placing the palm of her right hand over her heart. 'You guys really love each other, don't you? I thought love stories like these had ended with the twentieth century.'

'There are always enough love stories in the world to awe us. Ours is pretty straightforward, really.'

'I don't think so. It began with "I love you, pretty girl", remember?'

I wasn't aware of this until then—so Siddharth also fell in love with Sahiba at first sight?

Sahiba dismissed that with a wave. 'That was just a silly truth and dare game he was playing with his friends. How many times have I told you that?'

'Yeah, I know,' she said. 'I just wish I was there, though, instead of sitting at home with the flu.' She made a face, scrunching her tiny nose. Unlike her friend, Ginny's nose was sharp as an arrow.

'Ginny, it's been four months now. Stop fretting over it. Anyway, you are meeting him tomorrow.'

'I am,' she said. 'But you call me your best friend and I get to meet my best friend's boyfriend after four months! Very unfair, Sahiba, I must say.'

'Ginny, how many times should I tell you this? We met in November last year and started dating in January. He had this accident in February and he has just recovered. Tell me, where the hell was the time to meet?'

'Okay, okay,' Ginny said, holding her friend's hand. 'You're right, better late than never.' Offering her a wide smile, she said, 'I'm really happy for you. You've found your true love at sixteen. Look at me!'

'You grow up first,' Sahiba cackled, leaning ahead and patting her leg. 'Four feet, ten inches tall and thin like a straw, you're still a baby, Ginny.'

Ginny narrowed her eyes. 'Listen, I'm just a year younger to you, okay? And only a couple of inches shorter. Baby? What baby, huh?'

They both looked at each other and erupted in laughter.

Five

The next day, I went to Sahiba's school—Blue Angels, Vasant Vihar—and hid behind one of the imposing yellow-coloured school buses, waiting for her to emerge. I worked in my dad's electronic store and pursued a bachelor's in commerce through correspondence from Delhi University, so I had all the time in the world to do as I pleased. At half-past two, she breezed through the main gate, clearly excited about the afternoon.

The previous day, it was decided that Sahiba would meet Ginny, whose school was a few kilometres away in Dhaula Kuan, at the PVR Priya Complex, before their meeting with Siddharth. Ginny was excited. She had hugged and told Sahiba that she'd ask Siddharth a lot of questions about their romance.

It was a ten-minute walk from Sahiba's school to the complex. I tailed her and noticed that there was a spring in her step. She also looked prettier than usual—I could tell that she had made an effort to dress well: her face was bright and radiant (the pimples were still there, though), and her hair, nice and fluffy, coolly cascaded down her shoulders. I felt a pang of jealousy.

Ginny waited for Sahiba at the entrance of the complex. She could barely suppress her glee. When Sahiba came in sight, Ginny ran to her and asked with childlike enthusiasm, 'So when's he coming?'

'I just spoke to him on the phone,' replied Sahiba. 'He should be here in ten minutes, tops.'

'Great.'

They began walking towards the theatre and I followed them. Ginny poked her head inside a bookstore for a moment and then continued walking. I had gathered from one of their earlier conversations that she was very fond of reading books—classics, in particular—and dedicated at least an hour every day to reading one. She also urged Sahiba to give reading a try, told her it changed one's perspective towards life, but Sahiba didn't comply—she didn't want anything to do with books unless they were prescribed in the school syllabus.

Instead, she was extremely fond of cooking and had cooked Siddharth mutton biryani on one of their dates. I know this, as usual, through my eavesdropping habit. He liked the biryani a lot because I remember him licking the lunchbox at the end. Ginny had complained that day that Sahiba never cooked for her and this partiality would not be tolerated. So sometimes, when they met in the park, Sahiba would bring along some home-cooked snacks that Ginny would gleefully gobble up.

It was some time next year, if I remember correctly, when Sahiba expressed to Siddharth her desire to have her own bakery. I thought that was very cool. Anyway, more on that later.

From the theatre, they took a left, passing shops, restaurants and snack counters. The delicious aroma of freshly cooked momos wafted towards us and for a moment, the girls ahead of me considered sharing a plate between them before deciding against it.

They stepped inside the Nirula's outlet at the far end of the street. I have always been a big fan of the restaurant chain and loved everything featured on their menu, especially their ice creams, but the import of fast food from the West seems to have lessened its popularity.

Sahiba beckoned Ginny towards the stairs to her right. On the first floor of the restaurant, the first thing they did was to enter the washroom. When I reached upstairs, I took a seat in the corner, facing the wall. The girls came out a few minutes later and sat at the table behind me. My back almost touched Sahiba's as we sat waiting.

I know I may come across as a cheesy little bastard to you, spying and eavesdropping on the girl I love, who clearly loved someone else. But what else was I supposed to do? At least, doing what I did kept me closer to Sahiba, the only girl I ever loved, and that was enough for me.

Sahiba's hair smelt of oranges. I sat there for a few minutes wallowing in her fragrance. I imagined both of us on a remote island: white sand, blue water and no one around. She was sitting, legs outstretched, looking out at the sea. I sat behind her, playing with her hair. Then, a phone rang, and I was back in the real world.

Sahiba answered it. 'He's here,' she said to Ginny.

Ginny whooped with joy. 'Can't wait to meet him.'

A minute or two later, I heard a booming voice from behind: 'Hi, I am Siddharth.'

Although I could have turned to look at the man I hated so much, I did not. He wasn't good-looking in any way and, for some reason, he always smiled, showing off his ugly teeth.

At the age of nineteen—he was two years older than Sahiba—Siddharth's hair was greying at his sideburns, but he never bothered to colour them. He definitely wore clothes without thinking as they never matched (if you want to know how not to dress up, Siddharth is your guy to learn it from). I mean, who wears sports shoes with trousers? And his nails, my God, his nails! There would be a ton of muck under them. It was as if whenever he had to go somewhere, he would first find a heap of sand, dig his hands into it, pull them out, inspect and, when satisfied that enough dirt had settled under his nails, walk out.

There were many times when I wanted to shake Sahiba and ask her, 'What the hell do you see in this guy?' She perfectly exemplified the saying 'Love is blind.'

'And I'm Ginny,' said Ginny. 'Her friend, best friend.' There was a pause. 'It's so nice to finally meet you.'

He cleared his throat. A loud, dissonant sound came out like that of a donkey braying. 'Yeah.'

Yeah? Is that what you say when someone says they are happy to meet you, you donkey? No! You say, 'It's nice meeting you, too.'

Seriously Sahiba, this guy?

'Sahiba told me about the accident you had a couple of months ago,' she carried on. 'Are you okay now?'

'Well, yeah, just this tiny scar now above my right eye.'

'Thank God,' said Sahiba. 'It was a terrible accident.'

'I'm fine now,' said Siddharth. 'Forget it, Sahiba. Tell me, what'll you guys eat?'

Ginny asked for a burger, Sahiba settled for a chicken footlong and Siddharth said he'd like a non-vegetarian thali since he was very hungry. He excused himself and went down the stairs, towards the counter, to place the order.

'So what do you think?' asked Sahiba, when he was out of earshot.

'Too early, sweetheart. You'll have to wait for my verdict.'

Few minutes later, Siddharth returned to his seat. 'It'll take ten minutes or so.'

'Perfect,' said Ginny. 'That'll give us enough time. Now, Sahiba has told me everything about how you guys met. But it would be lovely to hear about it from you, too.'

There was a long silence, with perhaps uncomfortable looks being passed around. I was guessing since I was facing the wall and didn't want to turn to face that ugly donkey.

'Are you sure?' he finally asked.

Six

'You want to hear his side of the story, Akshara?'

It took a moment for Akshara to realize I had asked her a question. She gave a little shiver as if she was breaking out of a trance. 'Sorry, Harry, did you ask me something?'

'I asked if you wanted to hear Siddharth's side of the story.' Seeing her disoriented expression, I realized she wasn't even listening. 'Siddharth is Sahiba's boyfriend. You . . . you were listening, right?'

The park was swarming with people now. It was a beautiful August evening. Above us, a few kites soared in the crisp blue sky, some jostling for space, others content in their solitude. I caught Akshara staring at a solitary red-coloured kite with its tail shaped like fish fins.

'Akshara,' I said, darting my glance between her and the kite. 'Are you with me?'

She shivered again, shook her head and then looked at me ruefully. 'Sorry, Harry, I . . . I just remembered something. Last year, Mummy, Daddy and I were flying that same kite and . . . and . . . ' she trailed off, her voice choking with tears.

21

She lowered her head and tears dripped from her eyes like water from a leaking pipe.

I gave her time. She took two minutes, then wiped her face with her hands. When she looked at me, I felt half a dozen knots tightening inside me. Her expression was heart-rending. Big, pretty eyes with nothing but pain in them. She ran her hand over her face again.

'Sorry, Harry, please continue.'

'Are you . . . are you sure?'

She nodded.

'Do you like the story? Um . . . I mean . . .'

'Yes, yes,' she said, managing a faint smile, 'I like it. Sahiba Didi is so similar to me.'

I was taken aback. 'Similar? How?'

'I mean, like her, I also believe in God. Mummy also used to believe in Him. Sahiba Didi is so fond of cooking. You know, Harry, I also spend a lot of time in the kitchen with Shilpi Aunty.'

'Oh, that way,' I said. 'Well, nice coincidence, huh?'

'And I also have a golden retriever. His name is Zephyrus.'

'Zephyrus? What . . . what does that even mean?'

'It's a Greek name for someone with a warm disposition.'

'Oh okay. Good to know.'

'Even her friend, Harry—her name is Ginny, right? I have a very good friend, Mishi, who is just like her. She is so short and thin that everybody in the class makes fun of her.'

Then she began recounting an incident with excitement. Last month, she said, her class teacher had asked Mishi to stand up while answering a question.

The teacher said, 'Sitting and speaking to your teacher is bad manners, Mishi.'

'But Harry,' Akshara continued, her eyes glinting with excitement now. 'She was . . . she was standing. Ha ha! She is so short that Deepa Ma'am thought she was sitting.'

A giggle broke out of her and Mummy was forgotten. I leaned back and enjoyed the moment. Nothing else mattered to her then. Kids are so perfect. I wish I could be a kid again.

After her laughter died down, I asked, 'So you want me to complete the story?'

'Of course, of course, Harry,' she replied. 'I want to know what happens in the end.'

'So you want to hear Siddharth's side of the story?'

She shrugged. 'Yeah, sure. Why not?'

'Okay,' I said.

Seven

'Of course, I'm sure,' said Ginny.

'What do you say, Sahiba?'

'Go ahead, Sidhu,' she said. 'It'd be lovely to relive those days.'

Siddharth cleared his throat. 'Okay, on public demand, here it goes.'

~

We were playing truth and dare—my friends, Asit, Vivek and I. They had chosen 'truth' and had answered some lame-duck questions about this girl and that. I sneered at them, told them they didn't have the nerve for a 'dare'. So when my turn came, they told me, 'Now you show some dare, boy.'

'Okay,' I said. 'Dare.'

They shared a wicked smile. I leaned back in my chair after taking a bite of the chicken Mac burger. After classes, we would hang out here in Priya Complex as our college—Venky—was nearby. They were still thinking, looking around. I had known them for a year since I took admission for BCom. Nice, fun guys to be with.

Then Asit said with a jump, 'Okay, that girl, right there. Go tell her you love her and spend some time with her.' He looked at Vivek who nodded his head in approval.

I turned to look at the girl, who would later go on to become my sweetheart. She was sitting with two of her friends, Shikha and Diksha, now my friends as well. The girl in question seemed like the reserved sort. She was quietly sipping her drink while her friends did most of the talking.

She was pleasant looking, even attractive, but in an understated kind of way.

'But why "I love you"?' I turned back to my friends. 'I can go talk to her, no problem with that.'

'Show us some nerve, boy,' they said.

'Bastards,' I said.

I finished my burger, drank my Coke and walked up to her. Sahiba sat facing me; one of her friends had her back to me and the other was sitting at her side.

I cleared my throat. 'I love you, pretty girl,' I said to Sahiba. 'Would you do me the honour of having the rest of your burger with me?'

She scrunched up her nose and furrowed her eyebrows. The noses of her friends also wrinkled and the three of them cast me repulsive looks.

'Excuse me?' said Sahiba, her nose still in the scrunched-up position.

'Sorry, it's a game,' I whispered and folded my hands. I sat down and explained it to her. Sahiba stole a quick, furtive glance at my friends on my insistence and we talked for nearly ten minutes or so. I came to know quite a bit about her then. She was not very forthcoming; her friends told me most of it. I was right about my first impression of her: she was reserved. Through her friends, I got to know that her sixteenth birthday had passed just two months ago and that she was in the twelfth standard. I came to know about her family, including the dog, and her fondness for cooking. But there was one thing no one told me but I noticed anyhow: she was very conscious of her pimples. Most of the time she sat with the palms of both her hands pressed to her face and her nose, which she contorted in every direction.

However, I liked her. She came across as a person who was unfeigned. Some people do a marvellous job of hiding themselves behind fake smiles, affectations and a veneer of concern. Sahiba could do no such thing. Her big and beautiful eyes were literally the windows to her soul. They were very expressive and now I know this for sure, but even then, when I met her for the first time, I knew that they weren't able to hide anything: sadness, happiness, envy, nothing at all.

After the conversation, I thanked her and returned to my friends. They bowed in reverence.

A week later, we met again, although, this time, we didn't talk. Both of us were with our respective friends, walking around this complex and indulging in window shopping. I caught sight of her ahead of me. As we drew level, we shared a smile—a quick, fleeting one—but it was enough. I realized I more than liked her.

Then another week later, when I saw her again—same place, same friends—I walked up to her.

'Hey Sahiba,' I said to her and looked at her friends. 'Hey Shikha, hey Diksha.'

'Hey Siddharth.'

'I was wondering . . .' I proceeded with some caution. 'Would you like to have an ice cream?'

'But it's cold,' said Shikha.

'Sahiba will get sick,' said Diksha.

Then they burst into giggles.

'Ice cream, huh?' asked Sahiba. Then she shrugged. 'Okay.'

So we came here, to Nirula's, and ordered two hot chocolate sundaes. I still remember how great she looked that day. She had a pink muffler wrapped around her neck and her hair fell over her shoulders. Her eyes were busy, mostly lowered in the ice cream glass, as she carefully scooped out the correct mix of ice cream, nuts and chocolate sauce. But time to time she would lift her eyes to look at me, regarding me with kindness.

'What did your friends say that day after you came and talked to me?' she asked, looking up at me after a couple of minutes of silence.

I had a big chunk of ice cream in my mouth. I swallowed it quickly and the sides of my mouth stung with the cold. 'Oh, they were impressed. They thought I couldn't walk up to a girl and tell her I love her.'

She smiled bashfully and continued digging into the glass. I think an uncomfortable silence fell between us then, both of us not knowing what to say next. It was my first time and from what I learnt later, hers too.

'So why are you so conscious about your pimples?' I really couldn't think of anything else to ask and the silence was gnawing at me.

She ran a quick hand over her face. 'Excuse me? No, I'm not.'

'Yes, you are, and also about your nose.'

Her right hand flew to her nose quickly. 'No, I'm not. Why do you say that?'

'Because you're always pinching your nose and pressing it . . . for what? To make it sharper?'

'I'm not conscious about anything, okay?' She resumed indulging in her ice cream. Then, a few seconds later, she added with a smile: 'Okay, maybe, but only a little.'

'You're a charming girl, Sahiba, you shouldn't be.'

'Charming?' she asked. 'No guy has ever called me that. Come to think of it, no guy has ever called me anything. This is my first . . . er . . .'

'Date,' I completed it for her.

A flush rose to her cheeks. She bent her head just in time for me to notice an abashed smile spread across it.

She let it dissipate and lifted her head. 'This is not a date.'

'So then what is it?'

Wrinkles formed across her forehead as she thought about this. Her facial expression teetered between a smile and discomfiture. I let myself wallow in her embarrassment a little while, then followed it with a hearty laugh. I could tell she was relieved.

'Of course, it isn't. I am joking.'

After a moment of silence, she said, 'I know you were.'

'So what are your hobbies?'

She told me that she liked cooking and a little bit of music. She also told me that she was a staunch believer in God. If ever diagnosed with a disease, she was the sort of person who'd visit a temple first and then a doctor. Every day, she prayed for two hours in the morning and evening.

When my turn came, I told her that I was very fond of eating and so we would make a good pair. She blushed again.

Then she asked me about my family. My father died two years ago of a heart attack. One moment he was fine, and the next, his right hand clutched the left side of his chest and his face twisted in pain. A minute later, he collapsed on the floor.

Life is so unpredictable. We were discussing my future—the colleges I could join, the courses I could do and how he'd love to see me excelling in life—when he left me. Since then, I never think about anything, never plan anything and as a proverb goes, take each day as it comes.

My mother was completely shaken that day. But she is a strong woman. She almost resurrected herself. In the last two years, I haven't seen so much as a frown on her face. She quietly goes about her duties. She is a teacher in a government school and dotes on me.

Sahiba listened intently and reached out for my hand, squeezing it gently. Then withdrawing it, she began talking about her family. She said she had the craziest family in the whole world. Her mother was taller than her father and her elder sister was taller than both of them, and she, Sahiba, was shorter than all of them. She hated it. She said her mother and sister were so pretty and tall that all eyes darted towards them wherever they went. She felt she was ordinary looking. I didn't agree with her.

Their dog, Zibby, slept on the bed, and Sahiba's father slept on the floor, on a mattress, as her mother snored loudly.

When Sahiba's paternal grandparents were alive, they had harassed her mother a lot. She'd simply followed their orders and was not allowed to do anything of her own accord. So when they passed away, Sahiba's mother told her father that henceforth he'd have to do the same thing—simply follow her orders. 'No man will ever have a say in this house,' her mother had declared.

Her sister, Aashima, Sahiba told me, was four years older than her and could think of only one thing: getting hitched to the 'right man'. She was obsessed with the idea of having a perfect affair with a perfect man. When not into guys, she would write. She was studying creative writing.

'Interesting family,' I said.

'You've to meet them to believe it,' she said, wiping the ice-cream smudge on her lips with a paper napkin.

I raised my eyebrows. 'It's just our first date and you already want me to meet your family. You're very fast, Sahiba, I must say.'

She mock-slapped me, giving out a little chuckle. We rose and stepped out of Nirula's. It was cooler than before and dusk was slowly approaching. I walked her to the nearest autorickshaw.

As she sat inside after settling the fare, she said, 'I had a nice time today. Thanks.'

'Yeah, me too.' And before I could add, 'We should do it again, sometime,' that runt of a driver roared past me, leaving me choking in the smoke.

By the time I reached home, I knew I was in love with her. It was an easy realization. Love is easy, after all. I think people make it tough by doubting it, asking too many questions.

My mother opened the door. I apparently had a smile plastered on my face and somehow she knew. Mothers, I tell you. The first thing she asked me was, 'What's the girl's name?'

'What girl?'

'The girl you're in love with?'

'I'm not in love with anyone.'

My mother is a strong woman, like I said earlier, both emotionally and physically. Her hands are beefy and calloused, like that of a farmer's. She twisted my ear with her right hand and I blurted out in pain, 'Sahibaaa . . .'

She let go of my ear. 'Good. So you'll have something to eat?'

By dinner time, I had told her everything about Sahiba. She loved the part about her unwavering belief in God.

Over the next two months, until January, we hung out together at least once a week after my classes. I would bunk my last class and rush to meet her. It was bliss: falling in love with the right person. By then I knew she had fallen for me too. Like I said earlier, Sahiba isn't the kind of person who could hide her emotions.

One Friday evening, at our usual hangout place here in this complex, we were sitting on a bench, gazing at the sun setting behind the trees. Usually, Sahiba tied her hair with the same blue-coloured band; that day she let them loose. They danced a little in the cool breeze and, time to time, she tucked them behind her ears.

I turned my head sideways to peer at her and smiled. When she caught my gaze, she asked, 'What?'

'I think we have fallen in love with each other, don't you think?'

She rolled her eyes heavenwards. 'Wow, what a lovely way to propose!'

'No, I'm not proposing,' I said. 'I'm just asking you.'

'What are you asking me, Sidhu?'

'That have we fallen in love with each other?'

She turned away and shook her head. 'I don't know. Have you?'

'I think, yes.'

She looked at me and her eyes lit up with a smile. 'Great, but couldn't you find a better way to say this?'

I gave her a confused shrug. 'What better way? What do you want me to do? Arrange for a band playing a love song now, order for a cake and flowers, or have confetti thrown on us? You girls, you expect too much.'

The smile vanished and in came a frown, all in less than a second. 'Yeah, sorry, but for your information, girls are like that!' Then she turned her head all the way to the other side.

After a few seconds, she turned to examine me, my head and shoulders, and then she spread out her arms and a smile as wide as the Panama Canal lit her face. She lifted her head. 'What's that?'

Holding out my arms, I said, 'Well, let's see, small pieces of coloured paper . . .'

'Confetti!' Her hands flew to her mouth. 'Oh my God!' Before she could speak further, some soft music started playing from behind us. We turned and saw a group of four people—one each on a guitar, a banjo, a flute and an accordion. I couldn't recognize the music, but it was soothing, perfect for the occasion.

Sahiba's eyes, now brighter than the brightest star in the brightest constellation, looked back at me in both incredulity and amazement. 'Wow!'

Then a pot-bellied man came hurtling towards us, with a chocolate cake and a bouquet of red and pink roses.

'Excuse me, ma'am,' he said. When Sahiba turned around to face him, he said, 'Flowers and cake for you.'

Sahiba's jaw dropped open.

'Take it,' I said.

Sahiba accepted the flowers and brought them to her nose. 'They smell great. Thanks.'

The confetti had stopped falling on them by now. I got hold of the cake and thanked the pot-bellied man. I opened the box and, yet again, Sahiba's hands flew to her mouth. On the cake was a message carved in white icing, 'I love you, pretty girl.'

'I don't believe it,' she said. 'I honestly don't.'

I cut out a small piece and offered it to her. 'I really love you, pretty girl.'

She threw her arms out and embraced me. 'Me too,' she said.

I motioned the musicians to stop. They stopped playing and promptly left. I nodded towards my friends Asit and Vivek and they emerged from behind the banyan tree.

I released myself from her embrace. 'And these are my friends. They were responsible for the confetti.'

'Wow, Sidhu, this is great. I don't believe you did all of this. Oh sorry—,' she said and turned to Asit and Vivek. 'I'm Sahiba.'

Vivek smiled and said, 'We know.' Then he turned to Asit and they decided to leave us alone in 'our special moment'.

We hugged once more before she decided to leave.

As we rose, I asked her, 'I think we have fallen in love with each other, don't you think?'

She laughed.

Eight

Finally, the donkey stopped talking. I would have yawned at least a dozen times in their saccharine love story. All Ginny wanted to know was how they met and Ugly Nails—nice name, right?—took half an hour to recount it.

As he kept laughing while narrating his story, I got tired of all the melodrama. Didn't he realize that his laughter resembled that of a donkey's bray? I couldn't take it any more and hurried out, without looking back at any of them.

Outside the door, I stopped and felt a wave of emotion overpowering me. I sincerely hoped no one in the world should experience the feeling of losing their first love.

In the evening the following day, as is customary, Ginny and Sahiba sat at their favourite spot in the park.

I hovered behind them. This was going to be an interesting conversation and I didn't want to miss it.

'Okay, now tell me,' began Sahiba, the moment they sat down. 'How did you find him?'

'I think Siddharth is a great guy. He loves you a lot. It shows.'

This disappointed me. I was hoping Ginny saw what I saw in him: ugly nails.

Sahiba took a deep breath, placing her right hand over her chest. I could tell Ginny's opinion about him mattered a great deal to her.

'Thanks,' she said. 'I love him so much, Ginny, and this . . . this makes me so happy. I pray to God every day that we can be together forever.'

'Touchwood,' said Ginny, touching the wooden bench.

Behind them, I crossed the index and ring finger of my right hand. That shouldn't happen. I won't let that happen.

Few days later, after her school hours, Sahiba hurried to Priya complex. I followed her as usual and when we reached, Ugly Nails greeted her with a tight hug.

Even from a distance, the first thing I noticed were his nails—they were dirtier than usual. I looked around to find a heap of sand somewhere, but I couldn't. This guy was resourceful, he'd manage to find dirt anywhere.

They decided to unwind in a café. They walked a few metres, then descended down a flight of stairs to their right, proceeded till the end of the alley and stepped inside Barista.

I took a seat behind Sahiba as usual. I really hated looking at Ugly Nails. She was laughing over a joke that I missed. Our heads almost touched. Her hair smelt of a fresh fragrance, as if she had just got out of a shower after shampooing her hair.

Then she remarked, 'Your scar seems to have almost vanished now.'

'Not that it matters,' said Ugly Nails. 'But, yeah.'

'You should be more careful, Sidhu.' Sahiba's voice had taken on a grim inflection. 'God saved you that day but road accidents in Delhi are so common these days.'

'Yeah, God and the doctors saved me.'

'No, God saved you. The doctors managed to save you because God wanted them to.'

'Yeah, okay, but you know it wasn't my fault. I was walking and this car came out of nowhere from the other side and rammed into me.'

'Fault or no fault, you better be careful. I can't afford to lose you.'

'Aww,' said Ugly Nails. 'Love you, too.'

She didn't even say, 'I love you', you donkey!

'You know,' continued Sahiba, her voice now almost normal. 'I wonder why you love me so much. In fact, that day, you could have walked over and talked to Shikha instead of me. She's prettier. Or you could have picked Diksha—she's a smart girl. Why me?'

'Hmm, interesting question,' he replied and didn't say anything for a while.

Say she is the best or she is prettier, Mr Ugly Nails. What is there to think? I wish Sahiba had asked that question to me.

And if you can't answer the question, at least go and order something. She would be feeling thirsty in this heat, asshole.

But what that guy said is, 'You don't think very highly of yourself, do you?'

Sahiba didn't answer.

Ugly Nails went on, 'I think you are a great person, pretty, of course, and I find you very interesting. I mean how many girls you know bake such awesome doughnuts and cakes?'

Sahiba sputtered a self-conscious laugh. 'Thanks for that. But pretty, interesting? I think you should say that about my sister. She dates so many guys, so many guys. I always wanted to be like her . . . no, I mean, not in the dating-so-many-guys department . . . I don't think I can handle that. But I guess I always wanted to be smart and pretty and chirpy like her.'

'But you are smart and pretty and chirpy!'

'You think so?'

'I don't think so. I know,' replied Ugly Nails.

'I don't know,' said Sahiba. 'Aashima is so confident and so positive. She knows exactly what to do with her life. She has a dream—she wants to be a writer and is pursuing it. She writes every day. I don't even know what I want in life.'

'You like cooking, don't you?'

'Yeah, but . . . I . . . I don't have a dream. Nothing to look forward to.'

'Don't worry, I'll find you one.'

She gave a thin smile.

'And by the way,' said Ugly Nails. 'Did I tell you that that day when we first met, I wasn't playing truth and dare with my friends. It was a lie. I was looking for a reason to come and talk to you. You see, because, just like it happens in the movies, I fell in love with you at first sight.'

Nine

'That donkey fooled Sahiba and made her fall in love with him!' I told Akshara, anger mounting in me like it always does whenever I think of that day. 'Why didn't I do something like that, Akshara? I always wonder.'

The sun had descended and the sky looked beautiful, awash with deep and bright colours. Not too far from the sun, a light and feathery moon had appeared too, struggling to gain strength.

Akshara shook her head. She removed her palms from her cheeks and looked at me in a great deal of confusion. 'Yes, why didn't you?' she cried. 'In fact, why didn't you do anything? You said you wouldn't give up so easily on your first love. But you did nothing, Harry!'

'Oh, I did do quite a bit, Akshara. And some of it, I regret deeply.'

'Why regret? Everything is fair in love and war, right?'

A chuckle escaped me. Smart kiddo. She was looking at me for an answer, confusion clouding her face. I wondered if I should tell her this. She'd hate me for it. She'd go away, not talk to me. I did a bad thing. Horrible thing. And I have never forgiven myself for that.

'I did a bad thing, Akshara,' I said, looking into her eyes. At least I can be man enough to admit what I did. 'A horrible thing.'

'Really?' she asked, wrinkling her nose. 'You seem like a good person, Harry. Mummy used to say that when we do bad things, bad things happen to us.'

'Well, I'll tell you what, your Mummy is one hundred per cent right.'

'Was, Harry,' she said, frowning. 'Mummy was.' She lowered her head again, but didn't cry this time. A minute or two later, she cocked her head upward and said, 'Mummy used to tell me that there is heaven and hell—good people go to heaven and bad people go to hell.'

'Your Mummy is again one hundred per cent right— sorry, was right.'

'You know,' she continued, looking up at the sky that was now a perfect scarlet colour. 'I think Mummy will be in heaven. She was very good. She always helped people.' She paused, cleared her throat and looked back at me with determination. 'I also want to be like her, Harry. Maybe then I can meet her in heaven.'

'How did . . . um . . . how did she . . . she die?'

The tears that she'd been holding back rushed to flood her eyes. The sobs made her little shoulders tremble. 'We were walking and a car just hit her from behind.'

I cringed in pain. 'Oh God, was it a road accident? I'm so, so sorry, baby. I know someone who died in a road accident, too.'

'That driver will go to hell, Harry,' she declared, wiping her eyes. 'I know he will.'

After she composed herself, she asked me to continue. I decided to go back a few months in my story, when I saw Sahiba and Ugly Nails for the first time. But I was apprehensive—Akshara would definitely hate me after hearing this. Nonetheless, I decided to tell her everything.

Ten

It was January 2007 when I first realized that that giraffe—yeah, Ugly Nails had a long neck—had come in between Sahiba and me. I had seen them holding hands and gazing into each other's eyes not too far from our building near the old bus stop.

I cursed myself. Since I had never seen her interact with boys, I had assumed that she was not interested in anyone. So I held on to my feelings, waiting for the right moment. I was such a fool!

Without any further delay, I thought of at least letting Sahiba know that I loved her. What use is love if it isn't even expressed?

It was a Sunday. This was a week after I had seen her for the first time with Ugly Nails. We had an electronics shop in Khan Market and I had requested Dad for a leave that day. Despite being the busiest day, Dad agreed and didn't ask anything. He was a good father and always doted on me, just like my mother.

Sahiba was walking her dog around the building and fortunately, Ginny wasn't around. I decided to keep it simple.

My stomach roiled. What if she didn't even recognize me? I brushed aside the thought. Of course she would. She had seen me many times, we had even shared a few smiles and hellos.

Without further ado and before the negative voice in my head took control, I walked up to her.

'Hey . . . Sahiba,' I called out. She turned around. 'I wanted to . . . say that . . .' I turned my gaze to the dog. 'Nice dog. What's his name?'

'Zibby,' she said and nodded. Then we gave each other blank looks and confused smiles. She rubbed her palms and crossed her hands across her chest. Although it was January, it wasn't very cold that day and the sun was kind enough to shower us with enough warmth. 'Uh . . . what's your name? I . . . I don't seem to—'

'Harvinder,' I replied, grossly embarrassed that the girl I was about to propose to didn't even know my name. 'You can call me Harry. Harvinder is very old-fashioned, you know.'

She nodded again. More blank looks and confused smiles. Just when she was about to turn on her heels, a trembling voice came out of me: 'Would you . . . would you like to go on a date with me?'

She stopped, thought for a few moments and without looking at me, said, 'I'm sorry, but I'm . . . I'm not into guys, um, if you know what I mean. Sorry.' Then she walked away.

Her unabashed lie startled me initially, then made me angry. By the time she had rounded the corner to the left and disappeared from view, I was furious. Although I could have confronted her, told her that the giraffe that was looming over her that day was a guy, it wouldn't have served any purpose. On the contrary, I would have ended up antagonizing her.

I let the matter rest and thought of confronting her in front of that animal. I tailed them a few times but ultimately started wondering about the futility of the exercise. Sahiba loved Ugly Nails and Ugly Nails loved Sahiba. Would I be able to change that?

There are telltale signs when two people are in love: hands are held firmly, fingers tightly interlocked, the world around doesn't seem to exist and smiles are exchanged for no reason. It crushed me when I saw them doing this.

But how did this happen? How did I suddenly lose her? Till last month, I had it all figured out—I would slowly form an amicable relation with Sahiba and then ask her out. And now, in January, I see her with this dog—not Zibby—holding hands and gazing into each other's eyes as if nothing else exists. It isn't fair. I never even got a chance to try.

Somewhere in the first week of February, about two weeks after Sahiba had lied to me that she was a lesbian, I decided to give myself the chance I never got.

Winters were at their devastating best in Delhi. It was biting cold and my teeth clattered. I wasn't wearing gloves and automatically my hands were rolled into fists, nails digging into the meat of my palms. The afternoon was foggy; the sky an ominous grey, overcast. People milled around in leather jackets and overcoats. While some had their hands tightly folded across their chests, others rubbed them to dispel some of the cold. A cloud of white smoke snaked in front of open mouths.

I began my walk to the lovey-dovey couple to disrupt their peace. Ugly Nails was looking into Sahiba's eyes—fine, they deserved to be looked into, but why, really why, was Sahiba looking back into his? They didn't warrant that sort of attention. They were the most ordinary eyes you'll ever see—small and inexpressive. His eyelashes criss-crossed like railway tracks in the open field and the eyebrows were so light, almost missing, with a big scratch bisecting the right eyebrow. I could have cheerfully strangled him until both his eyeballs popped out.

Both of them looked up when I reached their bench. It seemed Sahiba had a thing for benches. Even out here, like in our park, she'd always sit on one. It had Nirula's to its left, dead ahead was the complex where the *autowallas* sat bickering about the rising CNG prices, to its right, down the street, were shops and restaurants. Behind them was a banyan tree that offered enough shade in the summer season. I thought they chose this bench because it faced west—one could view the setting sun in all its glory behind the tall buildings.

Sahiba pulled out her hands from his grasp and a look of dread, with a tinge of guilt, came on her face. She smiled foolishly.

'I thought you were a lesbian,' I said.

Sahiba emitted a troubled sigh. 'I'm sorry, I . . . I didn't know what else to say to you that day.'

'I . . . I'm sorry to interrupt,' interrupted Doggy. 'But why did you say you were a lesbian?'

'Because he asked me for a date!'

'A date?' he asked and frowned. The frown disappeared a moment later and gave way to a nonchalant smile. 'So what's wrong with that? You could have.'

Sahiba had big eyes, but when she stared at him with her eyes wide open, it appeared as if she only had two eyes on her face; everything else either went on a French leave or a little loo break, even the fat bulbous nose. 'What's wrong with that?' she squealed, mimicking him. 'Are you serious?'

'The guy clearly loves you,' he cried, waving his arm at me. 'You could have at least done that for him.'

One tear rolled out of Sahiba's right eye. It dropped on her cheek and settled there. 'What are you saying? And what about me . . . me and you?' She wiped the tear with the back of her right hand.

'Of course, we are together,' replied Ugly Nails. 'We'll always be together. But if the guy gets a little happiness from a date, it wouldn't hurt us.'

'Excuse me, hello guys,' I barged in. 'What's happening?'

'Brother,' said Doggy, with a pleading eye. 'I'm trying to help you here. By the way, when you know we love each other, you shouldn't ask her out on a date, right?'

'Thank God!' said Sahiba. The stiffness in her face disappeared. 'I was beginning to think you'd hand me over to every guy who comes to me.'

'No,' said Doggy. 'I was only trying to resolve the issue amicably.' Then he turned to me. Although his expression held sympathy that might have come across as genuine if we were discussing something else, I felt like punching him in the face repeatedly until I saw blood dripping down his nose. 'I'm sorry. I really don't think she's interested. But you are a good-looking man and there are so many girls out there!'

'Are you trying to make fun of me?' I asked.

'No way. Why would I do that?'

'Harvinder, please,' Sahiba said, her hands wide out to the sides as if to resolve the fight that hadn't even started. 'Please understand. We both love each other. I'm sorry I said I was a lesbian, but I didn't want to hurt you.' Then with her eyes half-closed and an expression evoking pity, she said, 'I'm sorry, but I'm already taken.'

Eleven

It had been three days since then, and I had told Dad I wasn't keeping well (something to do with a searing headache) and stayed home, in my room, the entire day. Although the room had enough to keep me entertained—a forty-two inch LCD TV, a DVD player, hundreds of movie disks, Xbox 360—all from our shop, I lay in bed either gazing at the false ceiling above or the wallpaper-lined wall across the bed.

I was thankful to God that we were rich, or rather, that my father was rich. I could spend my entire life doing nothing. But that's not what I wanted. I had told Dad many times to expand our business, but he was content with this one shop in Khan Market. He told me to do it instead. I agreed and planned to do an MBA from an American university after graduation. Although I could have done without it since I would never have to scout for a job, I wanted to educate myself and see the world. After that I planned to come back and expand the business, from one store to a chain of electronics stores in the city, something on the lines of Chroma.

Sahiba was also part of this plan, but now . . . There was a soft tap on the door and my mother peeped in. Seeing my eyes wide open, she entered.

'How are you feeling now, *beta*?'

'Okay, Mom.'

Mom was a strong-built woman of medium height with short, frizzy hair. I liked her; she never asked too many questions.

'You want to eat something?'

'Not now.'

'Okay, let me know whenever you do.' She nodded and left the room, closing the door behind her.

I sighed loudly and threw the blanket away. Getting to my feet, I walked over to the balcony. It was evening already and the birds had begun their trill. The leaves of the trees fluttered slightly in the breeze. In the park below, kids ran around. A few played on the rides on the right side of the park, some chased a dog. On the left side of the park, Sahiba and Ginny sat on their favourite bench. They faced each other and, even from this height, I could see Ginny rattling on and on. I wondered what they were talking about that day. Did they talk about me in the last three days? Was it a derision-filled talk or a scanty, forgettable one? But then again, I didn't know which would be better!

Last night, I came to a realization that Sahiba and Ugly Nails were in love; sulking over it wasn't going to help. The question was what could be done now. The answer, I realized, was nothing. Anything I did now would make Sahiba despise me. She didn't love me but at least she didn't despise me and that was a consolation. The thing to ponder over and take some respite from was that people evolve all the time, they break up all the time.

Okay, they love each other now, but few months later, a year later, who knows, right? I found on the Internet that an average relationship lasts only for a few months. After that, abuses are hurled and all the love disappears like magic.

I decided to wait for that time. For their inevitable break up. Till then, I thought of being a good boy and leaving her alone, greeting her with the kindest smile whenever I saw her and never again bugging her with the feelings I harboured for her.

Good plan, but there was only one problem—I was the most impatient person I had ever known.

Twelve

Few evenings later, I met them again. No, I didn't plan it this time. I ran into them, quite literally.

It was a cold, overcast day, but that hadn't deterred people, including me, from milling around in the park. Some jogged, others walked briskly, the lazy ones sauntered. Kids whooped and hollered. Dogs barked. And while looking everywhere else except at the path ahead, I bumped into a lazy couple. Them. My left elbow struck his back and the right arm hit her. They turned over instinctively, frowning.

'I'm so sorry. I'm so sorry. Oh Sahiba, oh Siddharth . . . sorry, I was looking somewhere else.'

Ugly Nails's frown eased. His forehead was still wrinkled though, perhaps wondering whether the bump was intentional. 'Don't worry about it,' he said eventually and smiled.

Sahiba's shoulders dropped. She crossed her arms across her chest and looked at me with suspicion. I didn't like that look. 'What are you doing here, Harry?'

It was heartening to know that she at least remembered my name. However, I knew what she was thinking—that I was a stalker, a pathetic freak who had nothing else to do but creep up on her and her damn boyfriend.

'Jogging,' I said, flatly.

They exchanged a conspiratorial look. The three of us moved a little sideways to our right to let the people behind us pass freely. Ugly Nails now had a sly smile on his face. I could tell what he was thinking: We know you were following us. You love my girl, don't you? But she's mine!

A strong impulse to hit him right between his eyes suddenly took root in me. I even imagined it as they both looked at me. The first punch would be soft, establishing the correct location between his eyes, and then the following punches would be harsh, as I withdraw my arm to get maximum leverage, and then: Bam! Bam! Bam!

'You can walk with us if you like,' he offered, breaking my reverie. In it, he had collapsed on the ground and Sahiba was trying to wake him up. 'I was leaving anyway, so you and Sahiba can continue your talk.'

Why does he do this, I wondered. He already had her, but he still tried to show off his kindness, generosity and large-heartedness—even pigs have big hearts. Maybe he was trying to show Sahiba that he was a great guy and make her feel that she did the right thing by loving him. He had done this earlier too: I'm so cool. You can be with my girlfriend if you love her. I don't mind. I'm a very cool guy.

This charade was doing another thing—insulting me. Of course, Sahiba would never really be interested in spending her time with me. So why would he say such a thing? To belittle me. Mock me. Maybe, both. Probably they'll have a laugh about this later.

But I wasn't going to lose this who's-a-better-person war.

'No, Siddharth,' I replied, with a smile so full and wide even my mother would never have the fortune to ever witness. 'I do not want to disturb you love birds. It's such a beautiful evening and you guys look great together. I think you should spend time together.' Besides, you guys will be breaking up soon, I guess, and then I'll talk to her, large-hearted piggy!

Sahiba gifted me a beautiful smile. She reached out for my arm and gave it two taps. 'Thanks, Harry, for understanding.'

I nodded lightly, took their leave after wishing them a great evening and resumed jogging.

Two days later, I met her in the elevator. There was no one else in it. When she entered, my heart did a somersault at the smile I got. She smiled with her cheeks fully stretched out like a rubber band about to give away. I smiled back, but only thinly.

'You live on the third floor, right?' she asked, giving me a sidelong glance.

I was hoping the electricity would go off for some time. 'That's right.'

'I see you in your balcony from the park.'

I nodded.

The elevator was slow. Only one floor had passed; there were two more to go. Deep inside, I wanted to flick the stop button and take her in my arms. But I was determined to show that I was not at all desperate. I wanted her to feel that I liked Ugly Nails and was happy that they were in a relationship. 'How's Ugl . . . uh . . . Siddharth?'

'He's fine.'

'Nice guy. You guys look great together.'

Sahiba looked at me, her head cocking just a little to her left. 'You are a nice guy too, you know.'

The elevator came to a shaky halt with a ding. For a moment, I thought I had got what I wanted, but slowly the door of the elevator opened, offering us a view of the park ahead.

We stepped out. The door behind us closed with a grating sound.

'Okay,' I said. 'Have a great day.'

She gave me her hand. 'Friends, are we?'

I intended to hold that hand forever, but right now, I settled for two seconds. Her touch was soft and heavenly.

'Of course,' I replied.

By the fourth week of February, the cold had begun to abate. The sun was out longer, its light brighter and warmer. Light, colourful clothes soon replaced winter woollies. At bedtime, I stopped burying myself beneath thick blankets and slept with the windows open, letting the silvery moonlight stream into the room.

By then, I thought Siddharth was done with his obnoxious little game and his real aversion towards me would begin to show.

It wasn't so.

He continued to greet me affably as if I were his best friend. He always invited me to join them and encouraged me to hang out with Sahiba in our park when he wasn't there.

I couldn't believe this guy. If I was him and Sahiba and I were together, I would have made sure she was miles away from the guy who loved her.

I'm sure he was no different, so why was he acting all goody-goody? Or had he adopted a reverse psychology? He'd have thought if he urges me to stay away from her, I would do the contrary.

I didn't know, so we continued with who's-a-better-person game. He acted good, I better; he acted kind, I kinder; he acted like he was concerned (told me once that he hoped I would find a great girl just like Sahiba), I appeared even more concerned. But in my bones I had begun to detest him—real vile, spiteful hatred—because I knew he hated me too. And every time he made a show of kindness and concern, he rose a few notches in Sahiba's eyes, making the likelihood of an impending break-up slimmer. By the end of February, my patience had worn out.

I did not plan this. I have always said this. I was driving my SUV down the road just a few blocks away from home. It was a normal day—there were a few school kids, several vegetable-sellers and a couple of beggars on the road. Ahead and to my left, I spotted him walking absent-mindedly.

Later, I would have plenty of time to ponder over the consequences of my action, but right then, I acted on impulse. I pressed down on the accelerator and timed the sharp turn to the left perfectly. The SUV jarred a little as it hit him and the impact sent him flying through the air. I came back on course with a full turn of the wheel on the right. The tyres gave out a loud, screeching sound. Then I pressed the accelerator fully to disappear down the street as fast as I could to ensure that no one saw the number plate of my car.

In the rear-view mirror, I could see a ring of people form around him.

Thirteen

In a flash and in a fit of revulsion, Akshara scooted away from me to the far end of the bench. Her hands covered her mouth in shock and she glared at me. I tried to move close to her. She retracted as much as she could in her crouched position.

'You killed him, Harry?' Tears lined her eyes again. 'You killed him?'

I tried moving closer to her again. She shooed me away.

'No, Akshara,' I said, her repugnance towards me breaking my heart. 'He didn't die.'

'You killed him!'

'No, I didn't. Are you even listening to me?'

'But you ran your car over him?'

'He didn't die Akshara. Listen to me!'

Her body shook at my outburst and I felt terrible yelling at her. When she was silent, I continued, 'Sorry, I'm so sorry. Okay, yes, I did hit him with my car, and I regret it deeply every day since then, but I didn't kill him. I told you earlier, right, that he was in the hospital and Sahiba would visit him, and that he was only left with a scar above his right eye. He didn't die.'

'But how could you do such a bad thing, Harry?'

I swallowed the lump in my throat. 'I don't know,' I said, shaking my head. 'I really don't know. I have been asking myself that question for the past nine years.'

'What would have become of Sahiba had anything happened to Sidhu? Did you ever think of that?'

I couldn't answer, couldn't even face the kid. She continued pricking at my conscience.

'Mummy used to say that before doing a bad thing to someone, you should always think how you would feel if they did that to you. How would you feel, Harry, if someone tried to kill the person you loved?'

I took a deep sigh. From the corner of my eye, I could see Akshara staring at me, expecting an answer. I had none.

'I'm sorry, Akshara,' I said, looking down, not having the audacity to look her in the eye. 'I really am sorry for what I did. But there's nothing I can do now to change any of it.'

When she tore her gaze away from me, I glanced at her. I could see the aversion in her face from the way she shook her head and moved her eyes. A minute or two later, she turned to me and asked me bluntly, 'Why are you even telling me this story, Harry?'

'Because . . . ,' I replied. 'Because, it will really help you.'

'Help me how?'

'Have a little patience, kid.'

She turned away again and fished out a tiny bottle from the pocket of her jeans. She unscrewed its cap slowly. Throwing her head back, she emptied its contents into her mouth.

'What's that?'

'Medicine,' she replied curtly, putting the empty bottle back in her pocket.

'What for?'

She took a moment to answer. 'Daddy made me see a doctor, a psychiatrist. He said I'm depressed.' She threw her hands up. 'Anyway, please complete the story. Shilpi Aunty will be here soon to pick me up.'

Fourteen

As soon as I hit him, I knew I had done something horrible. My throat went dry. I could feel sweat dribbling down my forehead and my hands were shaking over the steering wheel. All I remember next was that the engine had come to a stop and the cars behind had started honking. Then, silence. It could have been a minute, maybe a few minutes of silence, I am not sure. Then there was a loud patter on the windowpane to my side. Thud! Thud! Thud! I willed myself to look to my right. A bald, stout man, his face twisted in a grimace, gesticulated to move my car with sharp, angry movements of his hand. I nodded. Turned the key. The car did not start. I turned the key again. The engine sputtered for a second, then went dead again. After a few more attempts, I managed. But when I put the car in first gear, I released the clutch far too quickly and the engine died again. Outside, to my right, the man was screaming. More people were honking. I looked outside. My car was on the edge of a crossing. The cars behind couldn't go right, couldn't take a U-turn. I took a few deep breaths and then tried again. The engine roared to life and slowly and carefully, I took a right turn, avoiding the spiteful looks thrown at me from everywhere.

I stopped the car a few hundred metres away under a tree and killed the engine. Was he dead? I pushed back my seat and threw back my head. Did he recognize me? Did anyone else see me? I wiped my forehead. My eyes fell on the top mirror and I immediately looked away. Even in that split second, I could see fear, guilt and shame staring back at me. I couldn't bring myself to look into my own eyes.

And Sahiba thought I was a great guy.

There is a thing or two I know about karma. One, you sow what you reap, and two, a lot of people do not believe in it.

I didn't either, until five days after I had hit Siddharth, my car caught fire in the parking lot of a south Delhi mall. It was perhaps because of an oil leak. The door and windows got locked and no matter how much I slammed against the windowpanes with my fists, elbows, my phone and the cover of the CD player, the glass would not give away. As the flames zipped their way towards me and smoke filled the inside of the car, I started coughing. I struggled to breathe. I would die of asphyxiation first, I thought.

But I didn't.

In the end, I was burnt alive.

Fifteen

Akshara stood up in fright and staggered away from me. She was taking deep breaths as if her lungs were suddenly deprived of oxygen. Sweat poured down her face. She stared at me in horror, then confusion. She looked around and the flurry of activities calmed her down a little. She ran a hand over her face to wipe the sweat.

'You were what . . . what did you just say?'

'I was burnt alive.'

'Oh . . . okay. So . . . so . . .'

'Akshara,' I said. 'Don't be scared. I'm not a bad ghost.'

Her deep breaths returned and the horror came back on her face. She stumbled as she took a few more steps backwards.

'Gh . . . ghost? What . . . what are you saying, Harry?'

'What, you don't know this?'

'Know what, Harry?'

'Akshara, I've been dead for nine years.'

~

I didn't see Akshara for the next four days. I would go to the park and sit on the same bench, hoping to see her again. But she didn't turn up.

I enjoyed telling her my story and reliving those days. It's been such a long time. Besides, hardly anyone can see us, let alone talk to us.

You see, life is boring as a ghost.

That day, Akshara turned around and sprinted away from me, never turning to look back at me as if I were some kind of a rabid animal. I wasn't planning on hurting her. I just wanted to tell the kid a good story because she was sad, and I believed this story would give her a new perspective towards life, a new hope.

On the fifth day, I saw her walking on the jogging track with a tall, lean, handsome man—presumably her father. Her tiny fingers clasped her father's hand and she appeared to be at peace. Her cheeks were red with excitement of being with her daddy and her eyes happily darted here and there.

However, as soon as she spotted me, sitting on the same bench, the nervousness in her face became palpable. Her jaw dropped open and even from the distance, I could see her chest rise and fall with deep breaths. Her eyes didn't leave me. She blinked a few times and the horror on her face intensified when I didn't disappear.

She unclasped her fingers from her father's hand and quickly moved to his right, away from me. By now, the father and daughter had drawn level with the bench I was sitting on. I glanced a little over my shoulder and her father's body blocked her from my view. I couldn't tell what she planned on doing next. Just then, she threw her head back just a little to cast a furtive glance at me and instantly shot it in front, safely behind her father, when she caught my gaze.

The father and daughter left the park from the nearest exit and I didn't see them again until the next week.

This time, she was there with Shilpi Aunty. She was a short and stout dark complexioned woman who had a happy air about her. She treated the kid well, played with her, smiled a lot and appeared to be a good caretaker.

Today Akshara spotted me from quite a distance. But she didn't react. She completely avoided me. I missed talking to her. I wanted to complete the story. After a minute or two of vacillating, I walked up to them.

'Go, go away, Harry,' she said, without looking at me.

They were playing Frisbee and Akshara spoke to me when Shilpi Aunty had moved a couple of metres away to fetch it.

'I won't hurt you, Akshara. I . . .'

'Please go, Harry. You scare me.'

Shilpi Aunty saw her mumbling.

'Who are you talking to?' she asked, concern lining her forehead.

'Nobody,' Akshara replied.

'You sure?'

'Yes,' she replied, irritation filling her voice. 'I was just talking to myself.'

'Okay.' Satisfied, Shilpi Aunty took her position and threw the Frisbee at Akshara.

As Akshara bent to retrieve it, she whispered, 'Please go, Harry, I don't want to talk to you.'

'You certainly do,' I said. 'If you want your mummy back, come looking for me.'

Sixteen

The next day, Akshara came looking for me in the park. She was alone. By the time she reached, she was gasping for breath after her long sprint.

'You know where Mummy is?' she asked, between her panting breaths.

I smiled. 'Sit down, Akshara.'

She sat down at the other end of the bench, as far away from me as possible.

'Please answer the question, Harry.'

'So now you want to talk to me?'

She nodded hesitantly. 'But why . . . why can only I see you?'

'That's because you have a gift.'

'Gift?' she wrinkled her nose. 'What kind of gift?'

'You can see dead people.'

She lifted her right hand and slowly moved her index finger towards me. It went through and through. Of course, it would. I'm not corporeal, I'm just a damn ghost.

She withdrew her arm and fidgeted nervously. Creases formed on her forehead. A thin coat of sweat enveloped her face.

'I'm a good ghost, Akshara.' I moved towards her, but she shifted away from me. 'I will not hurt you.'

She ran her eyes over my body and her face twisted into a deep grimace. She swallowed and blinked a few times, then rubbed her eyes. I was still there. I let out the best affable smile I was capable of.

'I'm not here to hurt you, Akshara. On the contrary, I'm here to help you. Let me complete the story and you'll know.'

'You know, Harry, Doctor Aunty says you people don't exist.'

'What nonsense, Akshara!' I spat. 'Who the hell is Doctor Aunty to decide that? Just because she has some fancy degrees hanging on the walls of her office, she thinks she knows everything?'

Her grimace softened a little and she took a few deep breaths. 'My God, you're a ghost!' she tapped her heart with her right hand. 'When you were narrating the story, I did wonder a few times why no one ever saw you eavesdropping when you were right behind them.'

I smiled. 'Some of the perks of being a ghost. It's every ghost's favourite hobby.'

She wiped the sweat off her face. 'So all this time that you'd been following Sahiba Didi, you were dead? I mean that time when Siddharth Uncle told Ginny Didi about how they first met and . . . '

'Yes, Akshara,' I replied. 'I died on 5 March 2007.'

Silence fell between us for a while as she quietly absorbed all of this. Fair enough—the kid just discovered that her evening companion was a ghost. Slowly, her muscles relaxed and her fear dissipated. She asked hopefully, 'Can you bring my mother back?'

'No, of course not,' I said. 'I can't do that!'

'Do you know where she is?'

'I have an idea. Like I said, let me complete the story.'

She nodded slowly, hopefully. 'Okay, go on . . .'

She smiled and the spark came back in her eyes. She was the cutest kid I'd ever met and I really hoped this story would help her.

Seventeen

The last five days that I was alive, I didn't leave my house. I didn't know what happened to Ugly Nails, I didn't know what became of Sahiba. I didn't even walk over to my balcony, afraid I might find Sahiba crying in Ginny's arms. I feigned illness during those days and my parents, supporting and caring as they were, didn't press me too much.

I kept getting nightmares of Ugly Nails coming over to kill me, his face smashed and blood dripping from his head. I imagined him standing outside the door to my room and I'd be awake in a start, sweat dripping down my face, heart pounding in my chest, lungs working overtime to pull in air. After taking in deep breaths, I'd try going back to sleep. But he would always return.

It was only after I died did I learn that the bastard didn't even die. He only suffered injuries on the right side of his forehead and a few fractures in his legs, elbow and neck. I paid him a visit at the hospital; his right leg was raised, cast in bandages and cotton, and a cervical collar was tied around his neck.

I was with Sahiba all the way from home, right from the autorickshaw she boarded just outside the gate of our building for the twenty-minute ride to Batra Hospital. Her face was permanently cast in worry, deep in thought. Her eyes were pressed shut and the lips moved just a bit, enough to indicate that she was reciting prayers.

The bastard didn't even die. What else do you want, Sahiba? She didn't open her eyes. One of the drawbacks of being a ghost: no one can hear or see you except those with special abilities. Sahiba wasn't one of them.

After checking with the receptionist for Siddharth Sinha's room number, we took the elevator to the sixth floor. As we entered the room, tears gushed out of Sahiba's eyes. She ran towards his bed and planted a soft kiss on his cheek. He opened his eyes and smiled.

'Hey,' he said, apparently in pain, evident from the way he twitched his lips. 'You are here.'

'Finally,' she replied. She laced her fingers with whatever little of his fingers were poking out from the thick plaster on his right hand. 'Those donkeys you call friends, Vivek and Asit, were taking ages to confirm if they were coming. So I came alone.'

'You are not alone, Sahiba. I'm with you.'

Okay, yeah, I get it, she can't hear me.

Ugly Nails smiled a little before wincing in pain. 'Even smiling hurts,' he complained. There was a deep gash on his upper lip. 'My mom's here, by the way. She has gone to get a few medicines from the ground floor. I haven't told her about you . . . about us.'

'Oh shit.' She bit her lip. 'I'll hide then. How are you feeling now?'

'Alive. That's how I'm feeling.'

'May God punish that driver who did this to you. Bloody asshole!'

I clucked my tongue. You'll be happy to hear that God already did, Sahiba.

'I think it was a mistake.' He shook his head. 'It happened so quickly. I didn't get the time to react or see.'

'Anyway,' she brushed it aside. 'You're okay now. That's all that matters.'

There was a sound of the door creaking and Sahiba's hand flew to her mouth. Ugly Nails hurriedly motioned to her with his left hand to hide. From where I was standing, I could see his mother walking in to my left and Sahiba tiptoeing behind the curtains to my right. There was a wall to the left of the entrance, obscuring the bed, and that gave just about enough time for Sahiba to hide.

Siddharth's mother was tall and stout, she had sun-tanned skin and short, curly hair. She had a packet of fruits in one hand and medicines in the other.

'Had some rest?' she asked him, dropping the two packets on the table beside the bed.

'Yeah, Mum.' I could see the fear in his eyes. The curtain behind him was still fluttering.

'What happened? Why do you look worried?'

'No, no. When would I be out of here?'

She pulled out an apple from the packet and began cutting it with a small knife.

'Two weeks, at the most.' She put one piece in her mouth and in a plastic plate handed him the rest. 'You were lucky, always remember that. It could have been a lot worse.'

She fished out a medicine from the other packet and told him to take it after eating the apple. Then she looked into the packet again and after rummaging in it for a while, said, 'I forgot the receipt at the counter. Let me get it, else the insurance won't pay for it.'

I could see relief wash over Siddharth's face.

As the door opened, Sahiba came shuffling out. She dropped herself over Ugly Nails for a hug. 'Bye, bye, I'm going now. I love you. Your mother is right, it could have been a lot worse and I'm happy she said that. And that swine who did this will pay for it! He'll burn in hell! He'll suffer ten times more pain than you! He'll . . .'

Enough, Sahiba, enough. I get it!

A month later, in April, I followed them to Barista where Ugly Nails confessed to Sahiba that he wasn't playing truth and dare with his friends the day they first met.

Bastard! Why did that not occur to me?

From behind her, I got up and sat next to her on the couch, in the little space she had left to her right. But there was one problem: I was facing Ugly Nails now. He dug his dirty nails in the chocolate muffin and sucked on the straw in the cold coffee. There was an annoying slurping sound, as if the glass was empty, though it was filled to the brim.

'You fell in love with me at first sight?' Sahiba asked, incredulously. I could sense the exultation in her voice. It made her immensely happy. Ugly Nails didn't realize it. I knew her more than he knew her.

'Yes,' he replied. 'First sight. We weren't playing any game.' He winked.

She took a deep sigh and raised her eyebrows.

'Why are you surprised? I'm sure there must have been so many other guys hitting on you.'

'With all these pimples spotting my face and this big, fat nose right in the centre?' she asked, doing a great show of circling her face with her hand. 'No, you're the only one.'

My fists tightened. I felt a surge of anger within.

'Oh no, how can I forget Harry!' she said, tapping her forehead with her hand. 'He's the only other guy apart from you who liked me.'

The anger came down instantly, like a pressure release from a cooker.

'By the way,' said Ugly Nails. 'Where's he now? Haven't seen him in a while.'

'Me neither, might have shifted elsewhere,' she replied, raising her cup to empty the last few drops of cold coffee into her mouth. 'Nice guy, though. He was so understanding. Never made a fuss about the rejection.'

You don't even know that I'm dead, Sahiba? I used to live in your neighbourhood!

'I agree,' said Ugly Nails. 'Anyway, there are other guys too who find you pretty despite the pimples and your nose that you keep whining about. In fact, if you look through my eyes, you are the prettiest girl in this world.'

Eighteen

Eight months later, Ugly Nails met Sahiba's family. Since the past few weeks, Sahiba had been telling him that she wasn't particularly good at this game of cat and mouse, that she was done lying to her parents about her outings with him and that she was in love. She said she had never hidden anything from her mother and sister. Besides, they'd been together for almost a year now.

He had hesitated initially, questioning the need for it. He said that it was far too early, and that they were still young—seventeen and nineteen—but later conceded.

The meeting was planned on a Sunday afternoon in December. The evening before, he threw a tantrum.

'Is it really necessary?' he asked, frowning.

She had insisted that he should be at his best behaviour and be immaculately dressed for the meeting. She was never disingenuous in her opinion of his shabby dressing—the perpetual mismatch of them, the messy way in which his shirt was tucked in his jeans and the unwashed, unpolished shoes. So she had taken upon herself the task to shop for him that day.

They went to a mall in Saket and, after a quick coffee, started pushing their way through the crowds to get into the shops. Delhi malls are a mess on Saturday evenings. Even then, they managed to put together a good ensemble: a pair of plain blue denims from Benetton—Sahiba's choice, a crisp white shirt from Zara—Sahiba's choice again, and black loafers, also from Zara and yet again, her choice.

'I won't let you spoil my parents' first impression.'

'How would buying this change any of that?' he asked her. 'They would be more interested to know me rather than assess me based on the clothes I wear.'

She gave him a piercing look and he gave in like ice cream melting in the open sun. 'Fine,' he said, timidly.

'Good,' she said, visibly smug. 'Now we need to find you a nice belt so that you can finally tuck in your damn shirt.'

~

Sahiba's mother was beautiful, more beautiful than both her daughters, despite all the lines spiralling out of the corners of her eyes and disappearing just above her cheekbones. She had a sharp, distinguished nose and her lips appeared thinner than they actually were. Her shoulder-length brown hair was never out of place and she was always well-dressed. One look and she radiated oodles of confidence and grace. I'd never spoken to her, but always thought that she'd be a great mother-in-law for me.

Sahiba's father was a contrast: short and pot-bellied, he had a pair of old-fashioned spectacles set on his nose and a mop of unkempt, white hair over his head. I don't think he ever saw himself in the mirror, not even while combing his hair. He walked with an air of easy nonchalance, with his hands linked behind his back. He would nod as he surveyed the surroundings and smile at anyone who passed by— sometimes even a solitary, trespassing dog. The bulbous nose of Sahiba was a gift from her father.

Sahiba's sister, Aashima, was four years elder to her. She was a complete replica of her mother—smart, confident and great-looking. She spent a great deal of time on the phone. In the evenings, I have never seen her without a phone pressed to her ear. She would walk briskly in her skin-tight Nike lowers, her round, firm buttocks accentuated in all its glory. Sometimes she'd be screaming into the phone, other times casually jeering, but she always seemed to be in command of the conversation.

She changed boyfriends frequently—I know this by eavesdropping on Sahiba and Ginny—and was always in search of the perfect man. Sahiba had confessed that she was proud that she had found the perfect man at the very first go.

Ugly Nails was sweating when he reached the neighbourhood. The blue denims and white shirt brought an air of urbanity to him. The nails, however, were Siddharth-like: long and crooked, with dirt encrusted underneath them. He had shaved and combed his hair thoroughly, perhaps for the first time in his life.

He took a deep breath before entering the elevator on the ground floor. Apprehensively, he pressed the round button for the fifth floor. The doors rumbled to a shut. He rubbed his hands and looked up. I was standing opposite him, hoping it was I instead of him. I was also hoping

Sahiba's parents hated him, and that Zibby bore his sharp teeth into his skin.

I would have hoped for more, but the door opened on the fifth floor. We got out and waited outside Sahiba's apartment. Ugly Nails was still considering ringing the bell. Such a coward! I could see a thin film of sweat gleaming above his upper lip. I could almost hear his heart pounding inside his chest. He rang the bell. The ting-tong caused a flurry of footsteps inside, loud enough for us to hear. The dog barked.

Sahiba opened the door and said, 'Helloooo,' the 'o' seeming to extend endlessly.

The first smile of the day came on his face. 'I'm very nervous, honestly.'

'Don't be,' she said and led him inside.

I have been to this house many times—as a ghost, not when I was alive. So I know that it's a three-bedroom apartment, the first just at the entrance to our left. That was Sahiba's room. I have spent hours and hours in here watching her as she lay down, hands across her chest, looking up at the bare ceiling, with myriad expressions flitting across her face. Sahiba, I know now, loves to daydream. She can spend hours doing nothing, though I feel, sadly, that her thoughts mostly revolve around Ugly Nails.

When she was not thinking about Ugly Nails, she would read cookery books. Whenever the two would meet, she'd get him something she cooked. After passing out of school in March that year, she had joined a south Delhi college to study home science. Ugly Nails was inordinately pleased about it: along with a lovely girlfriend, he'd get lovely food too. I despised him a little more.

After her room, a passage led to a vast drawing and dining room. It was here, on the large L-shaped sofa, that Ugly Nails met Sahiba's father.

'Siddharth, Dad,' Sahiba introduced them.

Dad got up and the sofa squeaked. Zibby, who was sitting at the foot of the sofa, wagged his tail and then got up.

'What will you have, son? Beer?' Dad asked, offering his hand.

Ugly Nails took the hand but said no to beer. They both sat. Dad asked which part of Delhi he was from. He said he was from CR Park. Dad said that was close by, only a few kilometres away. Ugly Nails nodded.

I was looking at the dog; he nuzzled at Dad's leg. Shoo, shoo, Zibby, shoo. I was trying to catch the dog's attention and get him to bite Ugly Nails. I have read somewhere that animals are aware of spirits. The only thing Zibby did was sniff Ugly Nails's denims for a few seconds. Then he lost interest and came back to Dad.

Mom walked in then, along with Aashima. There were two more rooms in the house. The one on the right of the dining table was Aashima's and the one at the far end of the hall belonged to the parents, though I really had my doubts about that. Dad was always sprawled out on the sofa. It was Mom, I think, to whom the entire room belonged.

'Pleased to meet you, Siddharth,' said Aashima, sitting down beside her father. She was just out of the shower, I presumed; her hair was wet and tangled.

Mom looked spot on in her well-fitted denims and tight tee. Her hair was neatly tied in a bun. She was smiling.

'Hello Siddharth! How are you, son?' she extended her hand. Little green veins were visible at the back of her hand. Other than that, it was a beautiful, well-manicured hand.

'Great, Aunty,' he replied, the nervousness palpable on his face. After a subtle handshake, they both sat: Mom on the smaller side of the sofa beside Aashima and Ugly Nails on the longer side beside Dad. Now, only Sahiba was standing. And I stood next to her.

'Sahiba, get something to drink for Siddharth,' said Mom.

'No, I'm good, Aunty.'

'So what do you do, son, apart from hanging out with my daughter?'

Sahiba and Aashima smiled, Dad didn't. He was blankly looking at Ugly Nails.

Ugly Nails cleared his throat. 'I'm an actor . . . I mean I want to be an actor. Presently I work in theatre and am in my third year of BCom at Venky.'

Actor? Ugly Nails? How did I not know this until now? Perhaps I'm not a good eavesdropper. Or perhaps I don't do it enough. I should eavesdrop more.

'Oh, that's interesting,' said Mom. 'Well then, in a few years from now, you should be an actor, a successful, prominent one.'

'Actually Aunty, as long as I keep getting decent roles, I'm happy.' He looked at Sahiba and then turned to look at Mom. 'I plan to shift to Mumbai next year after completing my degree. You know, that's the place you should be in if you want to be an actor.'

'Mumbai?' asked Sahiba, frowning. 'You never told me
that. I hate that city. I don't want to go there!'

'Okay,' Ugly Nails replied, instantly. 'We won't.'

Aashima said, 'Attaboy!' Then twisting her face, in a
child-like plea, she said, 'Even I want a submissive guy like
that. Siddharth, you have any elder brothers?'

Ugly Nails said he was the only ugly nail in the family.

'Sidhu, I'm serious. We are not going to Mumbai!'

Dad cleared his throat. 'Are you guys getting married
now or what?'

A shot of embarrassment ran through Sahiba's face. She
clucked her tongue. 'No, no, I meant . . . er . . .'

'But you should have big plans!' cried Mom, earnestly,
interrupting her. Sahiba heaved a sigh of relief. She wanted
to thank her mother. 'Only if you have big plans will you be
big in action.'

'Oh, just let it be, Seema,' said Dad. 'Whatever makes
him happy.'

'But the boy needs the right advice. And . . .' She looked at
her husband in mock anger. 'You are not allowed to interrupt
me, you know that.'

Dad started laughing. 'Okay, fine.'

'I told you, right,' said Sahiba. 'That Mom's a little . . .'

'Dominating,' Aashima completed it for her.

'No, it's not like that,' Mom took over. 'See, when we got
married, there was this insane male dominance in the Sethi
family. I came from a liberal family, so my first few years were
claustrophobic. I couldn't even speak except in my room! For
twenty years I lived like that, and when his parents died, I
told him that it now had to be the other way round. So now

only I speak, and of course, my daughters. Men are allowed to speak in this house only when asked questions.'

Ugly Nails mimed if he could speak.

Mom broke out laughing.

'Of course you can,' Aashima said, waving a hand in front of her as if warding off a fly.

'Aunty, you just said men are allowed to speak only when asked questions. So I thought, you know . . . just in case.'

Ha ha, very funny, asshole!

'You don't worry, sweetheart. You are a guest. You can say anything you want to, unless . . .' She paused and glanced at Sahiba. 'Unless you plan to be with her.'

Ugly Nails hesitated for a moment, but when he saw Sahiba looking at him lovingly, he spoke out his mind, 'I do plan to be with her.'

'That's great!' Dad patted Ugly Nails's back. 'I'll have company then. And now that your nervousness is gone, how about a glass of beer?'

He said yes this time.

'Be quick,' said Mom. 'It's time for lunch.'

They had a glass of beer followed by lunch.

Nineteen

They met the next Sunday, Sahiba and Ugly Nails. I was with them too.

Since he visited her home, he was a constant part of the family conversations. The final verdict was: 'He is a nice boy', according to Mom and 'Devoid of any pretensions', according to Dad.

It thrilled Sahiba. She sat in her sister's room a night later discussing him.

'Too early to say,' Aashima said. 'But he comes across as a nice guy from what you told me. I like the way he proposed to you. I like a man who loves flattering his girl. But I tell you, if you really want to determine a man's character and his love for you, the best time to find out is after he's slept with you. Ninety-nine per cent of men change after that.'

'I wouldn't do that now,' said Sahiba. 'I'm saving that for later.'

'Well,' said Aashima, with a shrug. 'That's the second way to find out. If he's willing to wait that long, he certainly is the perfect man.'

'I know he is.'

'Guess we'll find out soon.'

The next Sunday, Ugly Nails was to perform in a play, *The Weird Couple*, in central Delhi's Vishwa Theatre. It was about a couple not in love with each other. It was adapted from a British play and was improvised to suit the Indian audience.

We reached ten minutes before the commencement time of 7 p.m. During the twenty-minute autorickshaw ride, I noticed that Sahiba was excited about the evening. She could hardly wait and asked the driver at least thrice how much time it would take for us to reach the destination.

Sahiba had never seen his performance, and after a lot of squabbling, he'd agreed that she could come and watch his play. This was last Sunday, at her home, when after lunch, they stood in the balcony, chatting. Ugly Nails was apprehensive about it. He said his skills were amateur at best. He wanted her to see him at the peak of his performance and felt that that would take some time. But she insisted and he agreed.

The autorickshaw rumbled to a stop. She paid the driver and we got out. It was a nice, sprightly evening, with not many cars or buses on the road. Some people gathered on the road across the theatre at a tea stall, smoking. There was a nip in the air, perhaps due to the December winds. We crossed the entrance to the theatre and were welcomed by large posters of the play all around us. There was a queue outside the ticket counter. Sahiba didn't have to join it, she had a pass.

She proceeded to the lobby, then to the man checking tickets at the entrance to the hall. I stood with Sahiba as she surveyed the surroundings. It was a small, neat, tastefully decorated theatre. On our left was a framed notice board with the schedule and show timings, along with scribbled notes by the audience and fans, appreciating a certain play and/or actor. Sahiba ran her finger on the notes to find one of Ugly Nails's. She found nothing.

Further left were pictures and clippings of people who had performed at this theatre and gone on to act in films. I spotted some old pictures of famous celebrities performing on the stage. It sure would be a boost for struggling actors like Ugly Nails.

After we stepped into the theatre, a man holding a torch, very much like in movie theatres, showed us our, I mean, Sahiba's seat. It was third from the top row, two seats to the right. Sahiba settled in. The seat next to her was vacant. Not that I needed it—I could have gleefully floated on top of her. But I took the seat; it felt as if we had come together to watch a play, like a couple.

The lights went out slowly and the murmurs died quickly. The assistants in front of the first row exchanged looks and settled to the sides. The curtains parted. First scene: Ugly Nails reading a newspaper on a bed with his onscreen wife at his side.

Blah-blah-blah. That is what went on for the next forty minutes. I was agonizingly bored and from the expressions of the audience—I was so bored I went around and watched their expression just to be sure—they were bored too. Sahiba was not. Every time Ugly Nails came on stage, she would watch with her mouth agape, as if Sir Shah Rukh Khan himself was performing!

After the show, backstage, Ugly Nails hugged her. He removed his proxy pencil moustache.

'You liked it?'

'Loved it.'

'My performance was okay?'

'Loved it.'

'Really?'

'Loved it.'

He took a step back and tilted his head. 'Can you say something else?'

Sahiba smiled and said that she meant every word, although she said only two words thrice.

'Coffee?'

'Yeah,' she said. 'I'd like that.'

They hailed an auto from outside the theatre. Ugly Nails sat with his legs splayed all over the seat. I couldn't find any space, so I sat on top of him. Sahiba gushed about his performance during the entire ride. 'You emote so well', 'Your dialogue delivery was so clear and crisp', 'Your stage presence is imposing', 'No other actor can match your skills', and so on. I thought otherwise. That was just love talking. It really does make a person blind.

He was mediocre. I could put that on paper, sign and stamp it if I could.

But I can't, so I rest my case.

The auto stopped outside the cafe, Coffee House, ten minutes later. The place was popular for its wide variety of snacks offered at reasonable rates. As always, the place was teeming with people, the banter loud and cheerful. People carried their food items from the counter to the seats, even as a long queue of hungry customers waited to place their order. Ugly Nails joined the queue and I gave company to Sahiba at the table near the wall.

As we waited, Sahiba kept gazing at Ugly Nails. He turned, saw her grinning at him and smiled right back. Then they continued grinning. Love can be irritating as well.

Ten minutes or so later, he returned with two samosas, paneer pakoras and two cups of tea. Didn't he ask her out for coffee? Sahiba didn't raise the question.

'I was thinking . . . ,' he began, after a bite of the samosa. 'Your mother was right that day.'

'About what?' Sahiba chose the pakoras first.

'About goals . . . that you should dream bigger.'

'I agree.' Sahiba was busy taking out the paneer piece from the pakora.

As there was no further comment on that, he asked, 'Did they like me, your parents?'

Sahiba nodded. 'I'm glad they did.'

'And your sister?'

'She liked you. But you know how she is. She said, "He's a nice guy but just wish he was more dashing."'

I sniggered. If I were drinking tea like him, the sudden sneer would have spluttered the tea from my mouth.

'Dashing?' he asked, and placed the teacup on the table.

What that meant, Ugly Nails, is someone like me.

A lean man, in his twenties, approached our table. 'Hey, could I use your phone for a minute? My phone's battery died.'

Without looking at him, Ugly Nails handed over his phone. 'Sure.'

'I know, I know,' said Sahiba. 'My sister craves good looks.'

He waved his hand. 'Exterior beauty is passé; inner beauty is the new cool.'

'You're implying that I'm not pretty, right?'

'No,' said Ugly Nails, with a contorted expression. 'I said I don't care about good looks, not that you are not pretty. You are pretty. But even if you weren't, it wouldn't have mattered. Like I said, exterior beauty . . .'

'Is passé,' Sahiba completed.

The lean man fiddled with the phone for a few seconds. I could sense something was wrong from the way he was eyeing the two of them, and before long, he made a dash for the exit behind him.

Sahiba shouted, 'Sidhu, your phone!'

He turned his head to the door. By then the man had disappeared.

I laughed at Ugly Nails. Inner beauty is the new cool, bro. Fucking hypocrite! Sahiba was gorgeous, the prettiest girl on the planet.

'What?' asked Sahiba, incredulously. 'You won't go after him?'

'It's all right, baby. Let him have it.'

'What?'

'Perhaps he needs it more than me.' He waved his hand. 'Anyway, he's gone.'

Sahiba rolled her eyes. 'Your SIM card is gone as well, and all your contacts.'

Instinctively, Ugly Nails scrambled to his feet, then sat down, dejected. 'Oh, I forgot that . . . I think it's too late now.'

'Afraid so.' Then she smiled, patting his arm. 'You're a good man.'

You are a dickhead, Ugly Nails.

Twenty

The truth is, howsoever I despised him, Ugly Nails was a good man.

That phone incident was a stupid, even cowardly display of his trait, but over the years, I learnt he was actually generous. He helped people whenever he could. A beggar would never go empty-handed if he approached him; he never haggled with auto drivers saying that they needed money more than him; and he actively donated money to charity. Every Saturday, he spent at least a couple of hours in an NGO close to his home teaching underprivileged children.

Once, almost a year after the phone incident, they were outside the takeaway counter of a burger joint in Priya complex. They planned to eat while on the ride back home. When the woman at the window handed him his burger and drink, a small child tugged at his shirt, stroking his stomach, indicating he was hungry. Ugly Nails looked at Sahiba and handed the kid his meal. A wide smile, of disbelief and exhilaration, came on the child's face. He thanked the two of them and sat on the small pavement devouring his meal.

He then turned to the woman at the window and said, 'One more meal, please.'

Two more kids now tugged at his shirt.

'Actually make that four, two for us and two for them.' The two kids thanked him profusely after getting their meals. When they were about to leave the counter, two more kids came running. 'Please, uncle, please, uncle, we are also very hungry.' Without a moment's hesitation, he handed them their meals. Soon there were four more, then eight, fifteen and then around twenty more kids begging him. He retrieved his wallet from the back pocket of his jeans and took out all the money he had—I counted Rs 450.

'Okay,' he said to the woman now, smiling hopelessly and handing her the money. 'Give me one meal and the rest please give it to these kids.' He turned to Sahiba. 'It's okay. I'm not that hungry anyway. I'll eat at home.'

'Ten minutes ago you told me that you were very hungry.'

'Never mind. Oh . . . do you have money for the auto?'

'I have around hundred.'

'That should be enough.' He passed on the burger and drink to Sahiba. 'Here, eat! I know you are hungry.'

Sahiba took it and passed it on to the youngest kid. The kid's eyes beamed at the food. 'If you don't eat, even I won't. Let these kids have a good time today.'

And they left the place, leaving the excited kids behind them.

One day, during winter the same year, he saw an old woman in threadbare clothes shivering by the road opposite the complex. Without even a thought, he removed his jacket and spread it over her shoulders and walked away.

'You know,' said Sahiba, when Ugly Nails returned to her side. 'I want to be like you and help as many people as I can some day.'

'It always starts with one.'

'I know, but I just can't get myself to doing it. I'm very self-centred, I think.'

'Maybe you need a push from the universe,' he said, throwing his arm around her. 'Some day.'

'Some day,' she repeated.

Few minutes later, they stepped inside Nirula's. 'Let's have an ice cream,' he said.

'You want to have an ice cream in winter?'

'I love having ice creams in winter.'

'Okay.'

At the counter, he ordered two hot chocolate fudge with extra chocolate sauce and nuts.

'I love this so much,' he said to Sahiba as the man at the counter handed him the two glasses.

As they approached the nearest table, Sahiba said, 'My bakery will offer such delicious pastries that you'll forget this.'

'So you are serious about opening your own bakery?'

'I am,' she said, scrunching her nose. 'You're the one who's been motivating me since last year. "Oh Sahiba, you bake so well", "Oh Sahiba, why don't you have your own bakery?", "Oh Sahiba, I know you can do it". Remember? I took your advice seriously.'

She winked and took a spoonful. A thin layer of chocolate sauce settled above her lips, not unlike the pencil moustache Ugly Nails puts on when he's performing on stage.

'And we are not going to Mumbai. I hate that city. It's so cramped. Forget your acting. Help me build my bakery, please!' Sahiba wiped away the pencil moustache.

'Of course, Sahiba,' he said, squeezing her hand across the table. Bastard just needed an opportunity to touch her. 'I've managed to save some money, enough to get us started, you know, for the initial rent and all.'

'Great, great,' she said, excited. 'I want to start as soon as I'm through with my college.'

'Oh, so we have time. Roughly a year and a half. I should have saved enough by then.'

He had been working in the knowledge process outsourcing industry in Gurgaon for the last few months. In the evenings and during weekends, he would find time for theatre.

'That is no nice,' said Sahiba. 'You know, I have even thought of a name for my bakery—Angel's Basket.'

'Sounds good,' he said. 'Sounds good.' He gazed at her in admiration. 'I'm so proud of you, Sahiba. You're the best. You'll soon have your own bakery at such a young age! Who does that?'

'Thanks to you,' she said.

'No.' He shook his head. 'It's all your effort and passion.' He scooped out the last bit of ice cream from the glass and gulped it down. 'So, pretty girl, any other boys hit on you lately?'

She snorted. 'Where did that come from? No,' she replied, thoughtfully. 'Not since that guy Harry.'

'Oh Harry, yes, nice guy. Where's he now?'

'Haven't seen him in years. Perhaps he's shifted to some other place.'

I wanted to hold her arms and shake the hell out of her. The girl didn't even know I died because of her, well indirectly, at least. Had I not fallen in love with her, I wouldn't have tried to kill Ugly Nails, and karma, with its long arms, wouldn't have tried to chasten me.

'Why do you ask, though?' she asked, while continuing to scrape the corners of the glass with her spoon.

Sahiba, talk about me with some conviction at least. After all, I gave my life for you.

'I'm sure you never liked him,' she said, finishing her ice cream. She set aside the glass and left the spoon inside it.

'Why would I not like him?'

'Because he was in love with me?'

'So?'

'So this: no guy likes if some other guy hits on his girl.'

'Who told you that?'

'I . . . I just know.' Her narrow shoulders closed in. 'You used to tease him, right, with all your concern? "Oh, you can walk with her if you like" and so on.'

Ugly Nails wiped his lips with the already used dirty tissue paper and placed the glass aside.

Then, in the most earnest expression, he said, 'Hell, no! I genuinely felt bad for the guy. It's sad if you love a person and that person loves someone else. Don't you watch Bollywood movies? Heartbreaks devastate me!'

'So you are saying that you genuinely wanted him to spend time with me.'

'Yes.'

'But why?'

'That's the least I, or rather we, could have done for him. I didn't want him to hate me for stealing his love.'

Twenty-one

If I was alive, I would have tried to kill myself. There was a time, almost four years ago, when I decided that I won't pester Sahiba, be a nice guy and patiently wait for them to break up, because break ups happen all the time.

Except in their case, it wasn't true. They never had a fight—really, they never fought. On the contrary, they were so close, so much in love, I doubted if even until the end of their lives, they would ever part. The closest they ever came to a fight was at her home, during an India–Pakistan cricket match, when Ugly Nails gulped down beer after beer with her father and Sahiba complained if he had come over to spend the day with her or her father. He then abandoned the match and they went for a stroll in the park. Their relationship was in its fifth year.

Ugly Nails had become a constant visitor in the Sethi household. He would usually drink a beer or two with Dad, talk to Mom, who always asked him questions about his acting, and get praised by Aashima for the permanent smile he'd brought on Sahiba's face. Even Zibby the dog seemed to like him; bastard never bit him.

In early 2011, Sahiba met his mother. The fact that her son had been visiting her home and hobnobbing with her family for the past four years, while she was only getting to meet Sahiba now did seem unfair, but her disposition suggested no such resentment. If anything, she was overtly exhilarated.

Their home was a reasonably furnished two bedroom-hall-kitchen DDA flat, although everything in the house appeared old and worn out. Like the sofa, especially the sofa. It was stacked in one corner, the swollen padding struggling to break free from the pistachio-coloured fabric over it. I could make out that the sofa hadn't been changed for years; the fabric over it, though, was changed a zillion times perhaps. Ugly Nails sat on it and the swollen padding conceded defeat but not without a squeaking sound. Sahiba sat next to him.

After serving water and refreshments, Mom-in-Law inquired about her general well-being and her family. Sahiba replied to each of them thoughtfully, and then apologized for not meeting her earlier.

'Oh, we did meet earlier,' said Mom-in-Law flatly.

Sahiba turned to Ugly Nails, slowly shook her head, then turned back to face her. 'I don't think so.'

'You remember when Siddharth met with that accident four years ago?' asked Mom-in-Law. 'Whoever that sonofabitch was who rammed his car into my son, may he die a rat's death. Anyway, when he was in the hospital, you visited him and when I entered the room, you hid behind the curtains, remember?'

Sahiba's jaw dropped, followed by Ugly Nails's. Her face turned scarlet and her eyeballs were on the verge of falling out. Both said nothing except exchange sheepish glances.

I wanted to ask Mom-in-Law what in God's name was a rat's death. Sonofabitch . . . okay, I deserve that, but why does she want a rat's death for me? Anyway, it's irrelevant. I'm dead and she'd be glad to know it was a very painful death.

'Come on, Ma,' said Ugly Nails. 'Why are you embarrassing us?'

'For fun, what else,' Ma replied. 'Just look at Sahiba's face, all red.' She got up and ran an affectionate hand over her head. 'It's okay, I was just teasing you. Come, let's have lunch now.'

They had lunch and a cup of tea after that. Then Ugly Nails dropped her back home in an auto.

I never thought I would say this, but those days I started to feel that perhaps Ugly Nails was indeed the right man for Sahiba. She was always happy with him, optimistic and cheerful about the future. When not with him, she'd either talk about him to Ginny, her parents or Aashima, or think about him and bake cakes.

The year was 2011, when India won its second World Cup after a gap of twenty-eight years. I loved watching cricket matches and if I had the company of someone who loved it equally, I enjoyed it even more. Weird as it may sound, that someone was Ugly Nails. That was perhaps the only thing common between us. No, the second common thing. The first, of course, was that we both loved Sahiba relentlessly.

At home, whenever he talked about Sahiba to his mother, he would have a bright glow on his face. I wished he did something about his nails, though—they were always a centimetre longer than necessary and covered with muck. But what I couldn't take away from him was that he genuinely cared for Sahiba.

On the day of the finals, I don't know what made him bring up a discussion about Sahiba's bakery. Sahiba's 'Angel's Basket' was to open next month, in May. He had saved money for the past three years to ensure it was a success.

They had rented a small place near Sahiba's neighbourhood in the popular C-block market. He had personally vetted the four employees who'd work there. He had supervised the laying of furnishing and arrangements at the place. For the raw materials, he had taken countless trips all over Delhi with Sahiba, after which a vendor in east Delhi near Mayur Vihar metro station was chosen. Together they had decided the menu—a fine assortment of pastries and cakes, few varieties of doughnuts, some Italian fast food, sandwiches and brownies—enough to fill two pages. He had got copies of the menu printed from a place close to his home. He had told her that the owner was an old friend of his father's and would charge only a reasonable amount. He even went around the entire locality within a three-kilometre radius to distribute the menus and announced with excitement that a new chic bakery was coming up in the neighbourhood.

He was very happy that Sahiba's dream was finally coming true.

'What about your acting?' his mother asked, just when the Indian batsmen reached the pitch.

'It's going okay.'

'I thought you never wanted a job. You wanted to go to Mumbai, right, to pursue your acting dream?'

'Yeah, Ma,' he said, eyes fixed on the television. The first ball of the second innings was about to be bowled.

'So?'

'I can do that later, Ma. Sahiba has never thought very highly about herself, and if she fails to do what she wanted now, she will never be able to do it again.'

'So you're giving up on your dream?'

'No, I'm just . . . I'm just . . .'

'What kind of a person gives up on his dream?'

He heaved a deep sigh and pressed the mute button of the television.

Hey, hey, bro, volume!

'Ma,' he said, a sense of calm on his face. 'Sahiba is my dream.'

Twenty-two

'Four chocolate truffles, eggless please, one chicken patty and that delicious looking brownie,' said the young woman to Sahiba.

Sahiba nodded to Harish, their assistant, or whatever his name was, who packed the items in a jiffy and handed it over.

'How much?' asked the young woman.

'There.' Sahiba pointed towards her right. Ugly Nails sat behind the desk punching numbers in the calculator.

'That'd be Rs 220,' he said.

'That's the best chocolate truffle I've ever had. Thank you,' the woman said, while making the payment.

Ugly Nails and Sahiba looked at each other and smiled. 'No, thank you,' they said together.

Now that's a fact: anyone who visited their place became a regular. Sahiba's pastries were really that damn good. Obviously, I never got a chance to eat them but just by the way they looked, I could bet my life on it. Sorry, just a figure of speech.

It'd been a year for Angel's Basket. The bakery was a hot favourite in the neighbourhood and since the past one month, they had also started taking bulk orders for parties and weddings. The staff of four had increased to a dozen. Sahiba had plans of expanding her business too.

Ugly Nails had quit his acting altogether. There was no time. He still had his job in Gurgaon though, for the money that he invested in the bakery. During weekends, he would help Sahiba. On weekdays, Aashima and Mom would help her. Dad was too busy doing nothing.

'I was thinking . . . that you should quit your job now,' Sahiba told Ugly Nails one day.

'What will I do then?' He was counting the money.

'Help me. I'll pay you more than your job pays you.'

'Oh,' he said, looking up. 'You want to be my boss.'

She winked.

'Yeah, I was thinking about the same thing.'

She cleared her throat. 'You know what Mom was saying last night?'

'What?'

'That we should get married now.'

He stopped counting and kept the money aside. 'And what do you think?'

Sahiba looked at the floor before gazing at him. 'That we should get married now.'

The two families met a month later at Sahiba's home. Mom-in-Law had got her an orange and magenta-coloured chiffon sari and Sahiba couldn't stop gushing about it. The parents' then proceeded to talk about their children's wedding without any further ado.

Sahiba's father couldn't stop praising Ugly Nails and said that he was the finest boy he'd ever met, and that his daughter couldn't have found a better man. Her mother agreed and then went on to praise her daughter. Even Ugly Nails was lucky to get her daughter, she said. Aashima got some homemade snacks and drinks for the guests. When his mother asked her about her plans of settling down, Aashima said she was looking for someone like her son. I swear I saw Ugly Nails blush.

'You really don't have a brother hiding somewhere?' she asked again, handing him a cup of tea.

'I wish I did.'

All of them laughed.

The wedding date was fixed. They were going to get married two months later, on 20 August 2012.

While on their way down, in the elevator, Ugly Nails's mother tousled his hair. 'She's a good girl.'

'I'm not that bad, either,' he said.

'Of course,' she smiled. The truth was he wasn't bad at all. The fucker just abandoned his own dream for her. After a thorough appraisal, I concluded that he'd make a better husband for Sahiba than me.

However, no one could ever find out.

Because ten days before their wedding, he died.

Twenty-three

Wherever he was, he would be thinking it was déjà-vu. The accident occurred on the same street where five years ago I had hit him with my car. Only this time, he succumbed to his injuries. The pedestrians on the street at the time reported to the police that they'd seen a white Fortuner hurtling down the road, driven by a bunch of alcoholics presumably, and hit a man just at the turn of the road. Death occurred instantly.

Although one would expect this should have pleased me, it didn't. I was sad; anyone would be if they'd seen Sahiba breaking down. Her mother passed on the news to her. Unfortunately, I was there to witness it.

On Sahiba's insistence, her mother had called up Siddharth's mother to discuss the venue arrangements. The phone slipped from her hand and crashed on the floor.

'What happened, Mom?'

When she said nothing, Sahiba asked again, the tremble in her voice not unnoticeable. 'What . . . what happened? Why are you looking at me like that? What did she say?'

Sahiba's father and Aashima sprang up from the sofa and joined her. By then tears were pouring down Mom's eyes.

'Is it . . . is it . . . everything is . . .' Sahiba tried to speculate.

But before she could, her mother hugged her. 'There was an accident and . . .'

Sahiba pushed herself away from her mother and faced her. Her gaze was downcast. Sahiba looked from her to her father and sister. Aashima was weeping by now. She knew. Dad's forehead wrinkled, his face shrunk in a pitiable frown. Even he knew. Sahiba ignored them. She turned back to her mother.

'Please tell me! What happened?'

Her mother gasped between her sobs, caressing her hair. She kissed her on the forehead. 'I'm so . . . so sorry.'

'For what?' Sahiba was taking quick, shallow breaths now. 'For what, Mom? For what? Nothing can happen to Sidhu, I know it.' When her mother continued to sob, pinching her lips and caressing Sahiba's hair, she asked again, her voice louder this time, 'What did she say? Please tell me! I know Sidhu is fine!'

Aashima dropped her head over her mother's shoulder. She tried to catch her breath between her sobs like an asthmatic. She linked her arms around her mother's waist. Tears had managed to find their way out of Sahiba's father's eyes now, but he made no sound, although blood seemed to have drained from his face.

Sahiba continued to press for answers. From where I was standing, I could see a pool of tears form behind her eyes, waiting to gush out. She swore one more time that Siddharth is fine, but she could sense the travesty of her own words and choked. She wasn't able to continue the charade any longer and the door holding back her tears was finally blown to pieces.

Sahiba fell to the floor with a thud, her painful and piercing wails echoing throughout the entire room. Aashima and her mother dropped to their knees. Aashima placed Sahiba's head in her arms; her mother patted her shoulder.

Sahiba wept in her sister's arms, while her arms punched the air and her legs trembled and fidgeted like that of a man drowning, desperate to keep his head above water. The weeps were interrupted only by her screams and her mother responded by patting and muttering, 'It's going to be all right.'

I left the family to mourn. Suddenly, I didn't hate Siddharth any more, and had it been within my power, I would have done anything to get him back to Sahiba. But I could do no such thing.

Before walking out of her building and entering mine, I thanked God that five years ago, when I had hit Siddharth with my car, he didn't die.

Had that happened, I would never have been able to forgive myself.

Twenty-four

A sudden howl from nearby startled me. It was Akshara.

'Why does this happen, Harry?' she asked, drawing deep breaths. 'Why? Why does God take away all the good people?' She lifted her legs and drew them close to her chest, and settled her head on her knees. She continued sobbing. 'You know, Mummy was also very nice. She . . . she always, always helped people, like Sidhu Uncle did. Even she gave up her dream for Daddy. She wanted to be an entre-entr-pre-entr-'

'Entrepreneur?'

'Yes, yes, Harry, that!' She wiped her tears. 'But Daddy said we would lose money. I don't know. Mummy was very kind, you know. She always helped people. She'd always give money to beggars, like Sidhu Uncle did. She would always feed the dogs outside our house, even the birds. She would always smile. Everyone liked her. Then why did God take her?'

I wanted to wipe her tears, but damn, my hands would just pass through her. A fresh bout of tears emerged from her eyes and she turned her head to the other side. She made no noise, but the rhythmic movement of her chest suggested that she was still crying. My heart ached for her, the way it ached four years ago for Sahiba. Death is horrible. It kills everyone around too.

Dusk was soon approaching and I decided to complete the story. I wanted to finish it as soon as I could. Perhaps the end would give her some peace.

'Akshara, Akshara.'

Her narrow shoulders continued to tremble.

'Please stop crying, Akshara,' I begged her. 'We can't change God's decision.'

'But why does God make such horrible decisions?' she screamed.

She looked at me, tears flowing unhindered from her eyes. Her big eyes blinked, hopeful, expecting an answer.

'I don't know,' I said, glancing at her forlorn expression. 'I don't know, Akshara.'

'Then why did he not kill me with my mummy?'

'Don't say that.'

She shook her head. 'I don't want to live without Mummy.' She uttered a cry of pain. 'I don't want to live, Harry.'

I moved close to her. 'You'll be okay, Akshara. Someday, you'll move on and then . . .'

'Move on?' she yelled. 'How can I move on? Did Sahiba Didi move on?'

I sighed. 'She didn't have to.'

She looked exasperated. 'What do you mean?'

'Er . . . something, something magical happened.'

She sniffed loudly and looked up. Then, she ran a quick hand over her eyes. 'What magical thing?'

'Can I complete the story?'

She nodded, sniffing and wiping her eyes again. 'Please, please do.'

Twenty-five

Since I died, I didn't pay as many visits to my house as I did to Sahiba's. There was a reason. Whenever I did, it pained me to watch my mother and father struggle to get on with their lives. I always thought my mother was brave and would be able to get through any of the troubles thrown her way, but not my loss. That struck her hard.

Even after years, the grief showed on her face. Her eyes still held the pain and her voice still shook when she spoke about me. My father did no better. He would pretend as if he was reading a book, sitting on his rocking chair in his study, but actually, he was staring up at my picture on the wall. That picture was clicked when he'd gifted me a car. I was smiling cheerfully, with the brand-new red sedan adorned with ribbons in the backdrop.

Their love would have been enough for me. I shouldn't have done what I did and perhaps had I not, I might have just been alive today.

I didn't see Sahiba for a week after that day, so I couldn't tell how she was coping. But I know by overhearing a conversation between her father and a neighbour in the park that the driver who killed Siddharth wasn't apprehended. It all happened so fast—witnesses at the scene of the crime echoed—that no one noticed the vehicle number or caught a glimpse of the driver. The case was shut.

Then one day, I saw Ginny walking over to Sahiba's building. It had been a week since I had been sitting in the park, looking up at Sahiba's balcony, but she did not come out even once. I followed Ginny to the elevator, then inside. The spark and happy gleam one would associate with Ginny's face were completely missing. Instead, she looked like someone who had recently lost a loved one. I never had a friend like that. I was a loner when I was alive.

She rang the bell and Sahiba's mother opened the door. The grim look on her face mirrored Ginny's expression. We entered. The house bore an eerie, disquieting look. The only sound was that of Zibby's paw hitting the floor as he ran toward us, and then his bark. A striking contrast to the earlier picture I had of this house: howls of laughter, Mom scolding Dad, Aashima screaming on the phone, everything bright and lively. For a moment, it occurred to me that this could have so easily been a different house, a different family.

The door to Sahiba's room was shut. Aashima joined us and they sat on the sofa; I stood, leaning against the wall.

As some inadvertent tears rolled down Mom's eyes, Ginny couldn't control her own and soon the three women started weeping.

'How's she doing now?' Ginny asked a good minute later, wiping her eyes.

No one replied for a minute. I presumed they didn't have an appropriate answer.

Then Mom opened her mouth, dabbing her eyes. 'Not good,' she said, and more tears rolled down her eyes.

Ginny scooted closer to Mom and squeezed her hand. 'I'm so sorry, Aunty. I wish I was here. I was in Lucknow, at a cousin's wedding. I just returned this morning.'

Mom nodded. 'Aashima told me.'

'She's in a terrible state, Ginny,' said Aashima in such a painful voice that I wanted to give her a long, warm hug. 'She hasn't been eating or drinking since last week. She's not talking to anyone, just lies in her bed, stares up at the wall, prays to God and sleeps.'

'And since this morning . . . I don't know what has got into my child's head,' said Mom. 'She keeps on muttering, "Siddharth will come back. I have faith in God. I had a dream there'll be a miracle".'

'Oh, she's expecting a miracle?' Ginny sounded alarmed.

'What miracle?' Aashima asked, earnestly. 'Siddharth's dead body was burnt four days ago. Sahiba was there, howling and screaming. If we hadn't caught hold of her, she would have rushed and jumped into the fire, I'm telling you. A *chautha* ceremony has been performed. Very soon, a *terwi*. His cousin brothers will soon immerse his ashes in the Ganges. He is no more in this world! How can he ever come back?'

'No, of course, I know . . .'

'I hope my daughter is not going crazy.'

Mom's whole body shook with another outburst of tears and she found solace in Ginny's arms. Ginny said in words that faltered, 'Nothing is going to h . . . happen to her. She'll be all right.'

Mom cried in her arms for a little while, then pushed herself away and stood up. 'I'll get some tea for you. Sorry, I didn't even offer anything to you.'

'Please, Aunty, don't bother. I just came here to meet Sahiba. Please, no formalities.'

'Come,' Aashima said and stood up.

Both of them walked over to Sahiba's room. I cast a look at Mom before following them. Her eyes were red and pudgy, the mascara smudged down her cheeks. She leaned back on the sofa and threw her head back.

Sahiba's room was dark except for a dim, orange light from a low-watt bulb on the wall opposite her bed. The curtain was drawn over the window so that no light from outside was allowed in. Ginny and Aashima proceeded cautiously to her bed. Aashima sat near the foot of the bed and Ginny sat near the pillow. Sahiba's face was on the other side, facing the wall. Ginny took a quick peek at her face, leaning over, and when she saw that her eyes were open, she turned Sahiba's body gently to her side. On seeing her friend, Sahiba sat bolt upright and embraced her.

'Where were you?' she asked and began sobbing softly.

'In Lucknow. I'm sorry. I'm so . . . so sorry, baby, for what happened.'

Sahiba pushed herself away from the embrace and somehow managed a smile. Aashima's face lit up like a candle in the dark. It was for the first time that she'd seen a smile on her sister's face in the past one week. But the glow on

Aashima's face dissipated as quickly as it had appeared at Sahiba's next words.

'He's going to come back. I know it.'

For a person who was unaware of the situation, the statement could so easily have been construed to mean that she was referring to a boyfriend who had left her for some other girl and that she was sure that her love would bring him back to her. Despite the impossible, there was sincerity and belief in those words.

'He's dead, Sahiba!' Ginny pleaded.

'I know that. But a miracle is going to happen and he'll be back!'

Ginny swivelled her head to look at Aashima, and I could discern a clear dread in her eyes. Aashima was on the verge of breaking down again. She lowered her head, slowly shaking it, dejectedly. Ginny turned to Sahiba.

'And how do you think that is going to happen?'

Sahiba gave a casual shrug. 'That's for God to figure out; I just know it'll happen.' Then she moved closer to Ginny. 'You know, I had a dream last night. I was at an unknown place: clear blue sky, bright sun, green fields all around, birds flapping their wings and singing above me, waves lapping against the shore somewhere in the distance and a slight wind from ahead blowing my hair. Then I heard someone call my name. I wheeled around on my feet. There was no one. Someone called my name again. I looked everywhere until I realized the voice came from above, somewhere from the sky.'

Sahiba wasn't looking at Ginny as she spoke; she appeared lost.

She continued: 'And the voice said, "Miracles happen, Sahiba. A thousand good deeds make a miracle!" The last line echoed for some time and when it died, I woke up with a start, shivering, and I knew what I had to do to bring Siddharth back. I remember Sidhu had told me once that you need a push from the universe to do good deeds. This is it, this is the push.'

Sahiba returned, from wherever she was, and looked happily at Ginny.

'So, I'll perform a thousand good deeds quickly and make a miracle happen.'

Twenty-six

I had left Sahiba for a week after Siddharth died, but now I decided I had to be with her, helping her in whichever way I could to bring him back.

When Ginny and Aashima walked out of the room, after unsuccessfully persuading Sahiba for a meal, they appeared dejected, sad and worried, all at the same time. Dad had returned home from wherever he'd been and stroked Mom's head on his lap affectionately, murmuring, 'Everything's going to be fine.'

From the look on his face, one could decipher that he was badly in need of such consolation himself. At the sight of the two girls exiting Sahiba's room, Mom sat upright and asked them about her daughter's condition, wiping her eyes.

'Same thing, Mom—miracle and he'll be back.'

'But I don't think that's such a bad thing after all,' suggested Ginny, taking a seat on the sofa. Aashima joined her too.

'How?' asked Mom, hopefully.

Ginny considered it one more time before answering. 'See,' she started, choosing her words carefully. 'I think it's a way of healing. Everybody has their own way. If doing good deeds helps her in believing that Siddharth will come back, what's wrong with that? In fact, she'll gain joy and satisfaction in the process, and she might move on.'

'But she'll be doing good deeds for the sole reason of getting Siddharth back,' Mom argued. I could hear the concern and fear in her voice. 'So how is it a good deed in the first place? Shouldn't a good deed be selfless? Anyhow, that's a different debate. More importantly, she'll expect Siddharth to be back once she finishes them—whenever that is—and if he's not back . . . What am I saying! Of course he won't be back, he's dead. Then what would happen? Don't you think she'll fall in a bigger pool of depression then?'

'Mom's got a point, Ginny.'

Ginny thought so, too. She didn't say anything more. I also agreed with Mom to some extent, but Ginny wasn't wrong when she said that Sahiba would get satisfaction from the good deeds.

'Can I say something here?' Dad cleared his throat. The three women looked at him. 'To answer your question, Seema—a good deed is a good deed, selfless or selfish, provided it helps someone. So let her do it, nothing wrong with that. No argument there. Siddharth, however, wouldn't come back. Of course, we all know that. But a very important thing would have happened by then—so much of time would have passed, don't you agree? Time is the biggest healer, and by then, most, if not all, of the pain would get washed away, like Ginny said, by the waves of joy. Maybe, by then, she'd have found a new reason to live—that of helping people.' Dad squeezed his wife's hand after slipping an arm around her shoulder. 'Our daughter is a nice girl, Seema. God would see to it that she gets out of this.'

Mom nodded slowly. I could see her relax a little, led by this new belief and hope. She opened her mouth to speak but no words came out. She swallowed. 'Do you . . . don't you think we should consult a psychiatrist, maybe?'

'Hmm . . .' Dad retracted his arm from around Mom's shoulder. 'Let me think.' He ruminated over this, biting his lower lip. When he was ready to speak after a minute or two, he appeared confident. 'I don't think so.' He shook his head slowly. 'At least not now. See, if we do that, Sahiba would begin to believe that we don't believe her. I'm no expert in this, but I feel that that will be a bad thing. Imagine forcing her to go to a psychiatrist! I mean, she'll never go of her own accord. A psychiatrist, although an expert, wouldn't think like a parent. They'll prescribe her strong medicines, may even suggest some activities. I don't know, but it might exacerbate her situation. I think we should wait and watch for a while. Let life take its natural course and let's monitor her. We can always consult a psychiatrist later should we feel a pressing need for it.'

Mom nodded, but this time firmly. 'Yes, yes, you are right. I agree.'

'What do you say, kids?'

'I think I also agree, Uncle.'

'Okay, Dad,' said Aashima, holding up her hand. 'But do you want us to play along with her? I mean, should we show her that we believe Siddharth would come back?'

'Not necessarily to that extent.' Dad replied. 'But we should be her support and strength now instead of thinking that she's crazy. We should help her in every way we can to help her accomplish the thousand good deeds that she talks about.'

Twenty-seven

'A thousand good deeds make a miracle?' asked Akshara, looking down, slowly tapping her forehead with her right index finger. 'I have heard about it. No, I read about it . . . oh yeah,' she suddenly remembered, excitedly. 'I read it on an author's blog. It was a short story, I think. But that was just fiction.'

'Are you saying you don't believe it?'

She considered it, gazed at me in confusion and then shook her head. 'No, Harry, how can it be possible?'

I smiled. 'Everything is possible, my dear, as long as you believe in it. I say it's all about your belief.'

'Did you believe in it?'

Now, I considered her question. 'Not initially, but later on, I very much did.'

Akshara nodded.

'Okay, and now, please don't interrupt me if you want me to complete the story. Look over there.' I pointed west, towards the sun that had just disappeared, leaving behind a fine kaleidoscope of colours. 'It will get dark soon. What have you told at home?'

Flippantly, she waved her arm. 'I said . . . I said I'm at Mishi's place. She lives in the same building as ours.'

'Mishi? Oh, your friend. And what if Shilpi Aunty goes over there looking for you?'

'I told Mishi to cook up some story.' Her eyes dilated. 'I wanted to hear your story.'

'Okay, then,' I said. 'Stop interrupting me if you want me to complete it.'

She put a finger to her lips and nodded dramatically.

The kids playing nearby and the group of middle-aged women chit-chatting in the park disoriented me for a moment.

'Okay, so where was I?'

'A thousand good deeds make a miracle.'

~

By late evening that day, after offering her prayers, Sahiba came out of her room without any coercion from any member of her family. In B-2/1033, Sangam Apartments, after an intense week of grief, hope and faith replaced the tears in Sahiba's eyes, and a smile, albeit small, adorned her pretty face.

Ginny and her family decided to play along, and soon, they started discussing their plans for the future.

Ginny said, 'So when do we begin our good deeds, Sahiba?'

'We?' Sahiba exclaimed. 'So you'll help me?'

Ginny squeezed her hand from across the dining table. 'Of course,' she replied. 'What do you think friends are for?'

'Thanks so much, Ginny. I love you so much.'

'All of us will help you, sweetheart,' said Mom, handing her a bowl of pineapple raita. 'Here, have some raita, your favourite. You must eat now. You have lost so much weight in the past week.'

Sahiba took it and ladled a serving on to her plate. 'Sidhu would be happy then. He never said it but I'm sure he thought I was a little fat.' She mixed the raita with the rice and put a spoonful in her mouth.

Mom looked at Dad, then at Aashima and Ginny, the tension in her face palpable.

Sahiba couldn't eat any more. She just moved the spoon on her plate in lazy circles.

She got up early the next day. I sat by her side on the bed the entire night. She slept like a baby, perhaps for the first time since Siddharth's death. After freshening up, she prayed for at least two hours, begging God to bring Sidhu back, before proceeding for breakfast.

At breakfast, Dad asked Sahiba about her bakery. She said Mom or Aashima could take care of it. All she wanted to do were the good deeds that would bring Siddharth back. Everything else could wait.

After filling her stomach with eggs and cereals, she bade goodbye to her family and headed out. Everyone looked perplexed and scared as they saw her leave. I decided to go with her in her quest. We took the elevator, waited as it rumbled down and got out of it on the ground floor.

Ginny was pursuing medicine from the All India Institute of Medical Sciences. She'd told Sahiba the day before that she would be able to join her only after her classes, in the evening. 'Take your time,' Sahiba had said. She could do this herself.

As we crossed the main gate of our building, I wondered what she was planning to do. It's one thing to know what you want, but quite another to know how to get it. She walked excitedly, looking here and there, watching people as they went past her. Then she stopped and looked to the left of the road—there were a few shops there, a chemist, couple of salons, a general store and a florist. She bit her nail. What the hell was she planning to do?

Nothing, apparently. She shook her head and proceeded with her walk.

'Need any help? Need any help?' she muttered to passers-by. People had different reactions: evasion, suspicion, indifference and confusion. But it didn't matter—no one took her help, no one even said anything. Who would? And why would they take help (assuming they needed one in the first place) from a complete stranger, and frankly, a weird one who went on chiming, 'Need any help? Need any help? Hey mister, need any help?'

This wasn't going to work. A thousand good deeds would take a million years this way.

A hundred metres or so ahead, a beggar—an old man with no teeth—was squatting to our left, holding out a tin to the people passing him by. Sahiba smiled. She unzipped the purse in her hand, took out a ten-rupee note and put it in the tin. The man thanked her saying, 'May you live a hundred years.' Sahiba stood there, wondering. She rummaged again in her purse and this time retrieved a hundred-rupee note. The old man's eyes lit up with wonder as she put that in the tin.

'Happy?' she asked.

The man, we suddenly realized, had teeth lurking in the corner as a wide smile parted his lips. He thanked her profusely with exaggerated movements of his arms.

Sahiba and I continued walking. 'The first deed,' she said to herself. But confusion suddenly enveloped her face like grey, ominous clouds taking over a clear, blue sky. She stood there, rooted in confusion. Then she spun around on her feet and taking large steps, the best her short legs could offer, proceeded back home.

She rang the bell. Mom opened the door and asked, 'You are already home?'

She entered and said, 'Mom, I'm confused.'

When prodded by her mother, she said, 'I was wondering if just giving away money is a good deed. I gave a hundred bucks to a beggar outside on the street. It felt good but suddenly it occurred to me that it was so convenient, don't you think?'

Before Mom could reply, Dad and Aashima came into the living room.

'What is it?' Dad asked.

'She's asking if giving away money is a good deed.'

'Don't you think it's too convenient, Dad?' Sahiba asked, walking up to him. 'I mean I can give hundred rupees to a thousand beggars, but would that be counted as a thousand good deeds? If it is, the rich can do millions of good deeds and can make miracle after miracle happen.'

As always, Dad took some time to reply, thinking over it. 'I think a good deed should feel good, bring one joy and lots of contentment at having helped somebody.' He paused. 'Did you feel that way?'

'I certainly did,' replied Sahiba. 'But it is far too convenient. I feel I should be doing something more, something that really, really helps people.'

'And what do you think that would be?' her sister asked her.

Sahiba shook her head. 'I wish I knew.'

'Fair enough then, if you feel that way, mull over it. I'm sure you'll get the answer. What matters is that it should feel right to you.'

'Thanks, Dad.'

She left them and ambled towards her room, saying that she had a lot of thinking to do.

By evening, she barely succeeded. She had a few ideas— volunteering for NGOs, doing charity work and working in government hospitals, but the conundrum was how would she do the math? How would she keep a track on the number? How would she know if the 'good-deed metre' passed a thousand or not?

She discussed this with Ginny as they sat on their favourite bench later in the evening. As usual, I hovered behind them, watching the perplexity on Sahiba's face intensifying as the evening wore on.

Ginny said she concurred with her father. 'I think when you do a good deed, you'll just know it.'

'You're right,' said Sahiba. 'But despite that knowledge, I've no idea what to do. I need help.'

Behind her, I smiled.

It was time for me to be of some help.

Twenty-eight

Before I go any further, I must tell you a bit about my journey after death.

So after my car caught fire, I pounded my fists on the doors and windows begging for help. The fire spread so fast that I could soon feel my skin melting away and my face shrinking. I still remember my last thought before dying—no man should ever endure the pain of being fried alive.

Then, there was a hard knock on the windowpane. The glass breaks. Right, I thought, so somebody has now come to help me.

I poked my head out through the glass. 'Yes?'

The man gestured me to step out of the car. I did.

'Yes?'

'Hello.' The man held out his hand. 'My name is Yama.'

I took the hand. It was cold and soft like a feather. 'Hey bro, I'm Harry . . . sorry, was Harry.' I looked over my shoulder and winced at my lifeless, charred body still wrapped in flames. I tore away my gaze and looked at this strange man. His face glowed abnormally, as if there was a light underneath his face. His skin had a slight bluish tinge and he wore a faded, loose shirt and baggy pants.

'What's bro?' he asked, wrinkling his nose.

'It's short for brother,' I replied. I ran my eyes over his body. 'Why is the colour of your skin blue? Are you all right?'

The man nodded. 'It's always been like that.'

'Hey bro, who did you say you were?'

'Yama, the God of Death.'

'Oh okay.'

'Do you know me?'

'I've heard about you.'

'Good things or bad things?'

'I can't say that, but you're responsible for people dying, right?'

'Aw . . . you have hurt my feelings, bro. That's an awful way to put it. I'm not responsible for people dying. Everyone has a limited time here. I'm just here to ensure that they don't exceed it. What I'm also in charge of, and it may interest you to know now that you're dead, is the journey of people after death. You know, putting them in heaven, hell or maybe an intermediate stage, and so on.'

'What's an intermediate stage?'

'You'll know all about it soon. Ready to get out of here?'

'Where are we going?'

'You'll know that, too.'

He snapped his fingers. The next moment I was standing in an enormous room and Yama was sitting behind a huge desk. When I looked around in awe, I noticed it wasn't really a room—there weren't any walls or even a roof, just a vast expanse of continual space. There wasn't any floor below my feet either, just a dense cloud of smoke. About a hundred metres or so to the sides, the smoke rose approximately to my height and coalesced perfectly to form a blanket of blackness. Beyond that, nothing was visible.

'Are we above the sky or something?' I asked Yama, who stood quite far from me, his face glowing much brighter than earlier, as if lit by the glare of an LCD screen in front of him. My voice echoed through the room, or whatever this place was called, and it boomeranged back at me from all directions.

'Of course, bro,' replied Yama. 'This is my office.' His voice, surprisingly, didn't echo much.

I slowly walked up to him. That it was all a strange dream, including the fire in my car, and that I might just wake up suddenly in my bed, did occur to me.

Nothing of that sort happened, though. I was actually there. My bare feet bounced on the white smoke and when I reached the God of Death, he was busy fiddling with a . . . a keyboard of what looked like a huge computer!

'What's . . . what the hell is that?' I came abreast of him and realized that my initial outrageous guess of there being an LCD screen in front of him was indeed spot on!

'A computer.'

'But that's almost as big as a theatre screen!'

No exaggeration there. Yama didn't respond and stared at the screen impatiently.

The screen glowed brighter than a thousand powerful light bulbs connected together. In the middle of it were two words:

Wait!

Initializing . . .

I dropped my eyes from the glare over to the keyboard. It was a strange one—big, of course, easily the size of the face of the centre table in Sahiba's living room. On the left were five rows of alphabetically arranged letters in a square frame and the seldom-used Z in the sixth row. In the centre was a shape that formed a strange kind of a . . . mouse! Yama glided the fingers of his right hand over this to speed up the process, but the two words continued to glare back at him. There were four huge arrow keys indicating the four directions on the right side of the keyboard.

That's it. No other keys!

Then, another word appeared on the screen:

Enter!

He brought his fingers to the left side of the keyboard and typed 'Harvinder Singh' slowly, then gave a little flick on that strange mouse (or was it the enter button?).

The screen came to life and fluttered—with a sound similar to a flock of birds flapping their wings together—and there appeared a list of people who shared my name. A total of 1008.

'What the hell is all of this?'

'Why?' he asked, with childlike enthusiasm. 'You think we are not technologically advanced?' Then he giggled. 'Some people from the software industry died a few years ago and I used their services.'

'When, fifty years ago?' I asked. 'You should consider updating this mammoth of a thing, bro! Maybe use a touch screen now and well, a smaller screen for starters.'

'Touch screen? What is that?'

'Never mind, Yama. There are more important things to do now.' I nodded at the screen.

'Oh, of course. What's your birth date?' he asked, and sheepishly added after a pause, 'You see, I don't do this stuff. My assistant does this. I just pass judgements later.'

'25 October 1988.'

'Thanks.' He typed the date on the right-hand side of the screen above the names. There was a flutter again; the names slowly disappeared one by one, until the screen was left with one entry.

This took time and in the middle of it, I asked Yama, 'By your assistant, do you mean Chitragupta?'

He didn't hide his surprise. 'Oh, you know him?'

'No, I've heard of him. Man, I thought you guys existed only in books!'

'No, bro, we're real.'

'So, where's he?'

'He's running some errands.'

'What kind of errands?'

He twisted his thick lips into a frown. 'You ask a lot of questions, bro. Some bad people died today. He's gone to drop them off in hell.'

'Oh, you mean hell is actually a place?'

'Of course!' he replied, looking at me as though I were some kind of an idiot. 'But trust me, bro, you don't want to see that place. All these baddies get a taste of their medicine there, so to speak.'

'And heaven? Is that also . . .'

He nodded before I completed my question.

'So where am I going?'

He looked at the screen. 'There! I have your name here. Now we're going to find out where you'll go—hell or heaven.'

He flicked on that mouse again (or the enter button) and the screen turned blank.

'Pay attention, bro.'

Over the next ten minutes, or twenty or thirty, I couldn't be sure, I saw my entire life flash before my eyes. I saw myself as a baby, an infant, a toddler, a school boy and finally the man that I had grown up to become. It all happened so fast that there were only flashes, yet enough to construct my entire life. There were some embarrassing sights too, like when I was caught peeping through the keyhole in Lara's room when she was changing. This was when we were on a school trip to Jaipur, and Lara was my first crush.

'Oh, naughty, naughty,' Yama said. 'You were a naughty boy, bro!' He winked. I smiled sheepishly.

Then there were sights I was proud of: being respectful to my parents and elders, and helping out people whenever I could. Once, there was a scuffle outside my shop one day, where a couple of men were beating up an old man. I intervened and helped him, but got beaten up instead.

And there were sights I was ashamed of—yes, I saw hitting Siddharth with my car too.

The last flash was of my car burning, and then the screen turned blank again.

Yama took a deep breath and sighed. 'Let's decide where I should be sending you now.' He thought for at least two minutes, his mind probably wondering if my good deeds outdid my bad ones, or the other way round. Then, he said, 'I can't send you to hell. You weren't a bad person, really.' I smiled, but it quickly turned to a frown when he said, 'Can't send you to heaven, either. That action of yours suggests malice to me. You must atone for it.'

So, an intermediate place was decided. In other words, purgatory, he said.

I'd have to expiate for my sin and cleanse my soul, before I can find a place in heaven. Yama decided to send me back so that I can live as a ghost until further notice.

'But don't be a bad ghost, bro,' he said, before bidding goodbye. 'When ghosts get bored downstairs, they resort to all kinds of nasty things. Remember, I'll be watching you from here.'

'But how much time will I get to spend as a ghost?'

'That I'll decide later, okay?' he replied. 'See, it's a boring thing to live like a ghost. I'm sorry, but I don't have a choice. But I like you, so if you get really bored down there and want some time off, or you need something, just utter my name five times.'

'Okay, bro.'

'All the best then, bro.'

'Thanks, bro.'

'Goodbye.'

'Goodbye.'

Twenty-nine

I thought I would get really bored living as a ghost, but surprisingly, I didn't. I used my time to eavesdrop, as if you didn't already know, and spend some alone time with Sahiba. Gradually, I began enjoying it. What I couldn't achieve as a human—being with Sahiba, looking at her up close, hearing her voice day in, day out, watching her sleep—I could as a ghost. Not bad a deal, not bad at all.

In her room, when Sahiba told Ginny that she needed help, I thought it was time to meet Yama again. I hadn't met him since that day as I never felt the need, but today, I thought I could do with some help from him.

I called out, 'Yama! Yama! Yama! Yama! Yama!'

Magic. I was at that crazy place again. It appeared darker than last time and the cloud of smoke looked thinner. Yama was behind his desk again, only this time his face wasn't glowing due to the glare of the screen in front of him, but due to its natural glow.

'Hey bro!' he exclaimed with joy. 'You're back!'

'I uttered your name five times, just like you said.'

'I know, I know,' he said. 'But after almost five years? How have you been, bro?'

'Not too bad.'

'Come here, come here. I'll show you something.'

I went and stood by his desk. In front of him was a smaller, cooler, slicker computer screen in place of that large theatre-like screen.

He flicked his fingers on the screen and the images moved. He zoomed in and out of the pictures using his index finger and thumb.

'See, see, touchscreen!' His eyes glinted like that of a kid presented with a toy. 'Recently, a tech guy died. He said he was the founder of a company that made fascinating computers. I got one for myself!'

I spotted the logo of a fruit that I never liked on the bottom of the screen. 'Good for you, bro.'

He toyed with the screen for a minute or two, then turned towards me. 'So what brings you here, bro?'

'There is a girl, Sahiba,' I began, wondering how to frame my words. 'I used to love her . . . no, I mean, I still do. She was madly in love with this guy . . . Ugly Nails, no, wait . . . that wasn't his real name . . . what was his name . . . Sinha, yeah, Siddharth Sinha. But he died last week and she is devastated. Now, yesterday, she had a dream. She believes that if she does a thousand good deeds, he'll somehow come back.'

'That's impossible!'

'No, let me complete . . . wait, what did you say?'

'It's impossible!' he spat again. 'If he's dead, he'll never come back! That girl is a fool, tell her that. I do remember this guy, though. Wonderful, truly remarkable guy. Never got a

foot wrong. I sent him over to heaven without a thought—
he's never coming back from there!'

'But, please, she'll die . . .'

'Bro, please, that's the protocol here.' He shook his head.
'Wait, is that what you came here for? To ask me to make a
dead man alive?'

I nodded awkwardly.

'Sorry, bro, not possible.'

'Please.'

'No, bro.'

'Please, please, bro.'

'Bro, I said no.'

I gave out a disappointed sigh. 'Fine, but I still want to
help that girl. Maybe the good deeds will help her move on
eventually. Can you at least make me visible to her?'

He gave me a slightly lopsided gaze, pushing his head
back a little.

'Okay, I'm willing to honour that.' He placed the palm
of his right hand over my chest, closed his eyes and muttered
a few words. 'Okay, she'll be able to see you now. But
nothing is going to change my decision. You tell her that.
Ugly Nails . . . no, wait . . . Siddharth Sinha is never coming
back, bro.'

Thirty

'You're kidding, right?' Akshara asked, scrunching up her nose.

'What?' I said, irritated at the kiddo interrupting me again.

She held out her arms. 'Yama? Chitragupta?' She scrunched up her nose again.

'What about them?'

'They exist only in books and movies. They're not real.'

I gave out a helpless sigh and slumped back. 'Who told you that?'

'No, I mean, Mummy had told me about them once. I think she told me a fantasy story about them. But that's what it was—a fantasy story.'

'Akshara, they do exist.'

She eyed me sceptically and scratched her head. 'Really?'

'I told you earlier, right, it's all about your belief. See, as I see it, the world is divided into cynics and believers. What matters is which group you come under.'

She thought about the question. Then she looked at me, determined and sure. 'A believer.'

'Good,' I said. 'Then believe me. I'm not lying, Akshara. I won't lie to you.'

'No, no, Harry,' she said, extending her hand towards me. It went through me. She smiled and pulled it back. 'I didn't mean that you're lying. I believe you.'

I looked in her eyes. 'You want me to continue?'

She bit her lip. 'Actually, one . . . one more question.'

'Hmm.'

'If you loved Sahiba Didi so much, why were you helping her to bring Ugl . . . oh no . . . Sidhu Uncle back? You hated him, right?'

Something tightened in my chest. I said, 'I always thought love was a game. You got to win it. But love is not a game. Love is sacrifice. Love is letting go. And above all, love is dreaming the impossible, like bringing back a dead man.'

~

Before meeting Sahiba, I looked at myself in the glass door at the entrance to her flat. I could faintly see my reflection. Oh, I still looked handsome. I hand-combed my hair and settled them nicely over my head. A few strands fell over my forehead. Never mind, it added to my charm. I had to look good. I was meeting her after five years.

I raised my arm to ring the bell, then shook my head foolishly. I bent forward, letting my upper body pass through the door and looked around. There was silence. Everyone appeared to be in their respective rooms. I got my entire body inside. Sahiba's room was shut. Again, I let my upper body pass through it. Oh, there she was, lying on the bed. Good. I got my body out and surveyed the other rooms.

The grandfather's clock in the living room chimed midnight. I found Sahiba's parents sleeping in the master bedroom, Zibby at the foot of the bed. Aashima snored loudly in her room. Satisfied, I proceeded back to Sahiba's room. I entered. Her head faced the other side.

'Sahiba,' I called out softly.

Like a whiplash, she turned her head. She was awake. 'Harry . . . Harry, what are you doing here? Wait, how did you come in? And where . . . where have you been all these years?'

I sat on the bed. Sahiba sat up too, impatiently looking at me, her hair a complete mess.

'There are so many things to tell you,' I began. Here's what I told her:

a) I died five years ago. Before saying it, I had asked her to press her mouth shut with both her hands to avoid a scream. Girls love screaming.

b) So, yes, if I had died, I was a ghost. Sorry about that.

c) I was here to help her. With her good deeds. To bring Ugl . . . Siddharth back. I didn't tell her what my bro from above had said.

d) Only she could see me.

e) But I told her not to tell anyone that. People would think she were crazy.

'Okay, you can take off your hands now. You won't scream, right?'

Slowly, she shook her head and removed her hands. Her mouth fell open and her jaw dropped all the way down to the collar of her red T-shirt. Her eyes had become the size of a watermelon. She cringed a little.

'Are you . . . are you serious, Harry?'

'How do you think I got through that door? And how do you think I know about Siddharth and your good deeds to bring him back?'

Her right hand flew to her mouth again. She moved back a little more. 'So you'd been . . . hovering around me all this while?'

'Hov . . . hovering around you? No, no, what makes you say that?'

She eyed me suspiciously. 'Harry?'

'Yeah, but only sometimes, and certainly not when Siddharth and you were alone.'

'You were also there when Siddharth and I used to be alone?'

I looked away. 'Only sometimes.'

'You bad, bad . . . ghost.'

Then we hugged. I didn't initiate it. She threw her arms around my neck and although it went through it, it felt great. She laughed and I joined her.

We retreated and Sahiba gave me a close-lipped smile. She told me about her confusion regarding the good deeds and I told her I knew about that as well.

'Do you have any idea what we could do?' she asked me.

'Not at the moment.'

'But you do believe me, right, that he'll come back after I accomplish them? That a thousand good deeds can make a miracle?' Her eyes were hopeful, and I could tell my answer mattered a great deal to her.

I didn't want to lie, but I couldn't say the truth either. That would devastate her. Her father's words rang loud and clear in my head—time is the best healer—and I believed that. I also believed that through the good deeds she might get a new reason to live, that she might move on, and I did not want to take that away from her.

'Yes,' I said. 'I do believe you.'

She gave her close-lipped smile again. Then a strange thought entered my mind: what if I was alive? Would I have a chance with Sahiba then? The thought promptly left. You're dead, Harry. Now help the girl find her love.

'But what can I do? I'm so confused. I want to do this as soon as possible and bring Siddharth back.'

'We'll find a way, Sahiba.'

She nodded and was soon lost in her thoughts. 'Don't you have some powers? I mean, you're a ghost, right? Ghosts have powers.'

I glanced at her in confusion. 'What powers?'

'Like they show in movies all the time.'

I shook my head. 'No, I don't have any powers. Sorry.'

'Oh,' she clucked her tongue and raked a hand through her hair. 'Maybe if you could hear someone's suffering or pain, I could go help them out.'

'Sounds good but I don't have that kind of power, Sahiba.'

'Wish you had, though. We could have done so many good deeds in a short span of time.'

'Actually,' I said, with a sudden flash of insight. 'Just give me some time.'

I closed my eyes and said, 'Yama! Yama! Yama! Yama! Yama!'

Thirty-one

'Look who is back!' Yama shrieked. 'It's my bro!'

Yama was at his desk again. This time I landed very close to him. There was a shorter man standing beside him. He didn't look much different from Yama in terms of the bluish tinge of the skin and the ethereal glow on the face, but he had longer hair, like that of a woman, reaching his shoulders. He had a slightly crooked back, perhaps caused by too much bending.

'This is Chitragupta,' Yama said. 'My assistant.'

'Hey dude.' I offered him my hand. 'I'm Harry . . . sorry, was Harry. I always forget that.'

Chitragupta shook it. 'What does "dude" mean?' His voice was husky and cut through the air.

'Dude means fellow, friend or mate.'

'Okay, d . . . dude. But my Lord told me your name was Harvinder.'

'Yeah, but Harry is shorter and cooler. Harvinder is like . . . yeah, like Chitragupta. It's so boring and outdated, dude.'

Chitragupta nodded. 'You're right, dude.'

'Okay, you carry on,' said Yama to Chitragupta. 'Increase the temperature setting in hell like we discussed. Let those buggers burn in hell, so to speak . . . oh . . . actually, literally.' He then gave out an insanely boisterous laugh.

'At once, my Lord.'

'Bye, dude,' Chitragupta said to me and promptly left, disappearing in the smoke to our right.

'So, bro, what brings you here?'

'How's your computer?'

'Oh, it's such a fantastic equipment! It has made my life so easy, bro. Thanks to you. When you derided my earlier computer, I decided to change it.'

'Mention not, bro.' I said. 'Hey, I was wondering if I could ask you a favour.'

'Of course, bro, as long as it's not about bringing Siddharth back to life.' He chuckled a little.

'No, no, I . . . I was wondering if there is a way I can hear er . . . the pain or suffering of the people around me, so . . . so I can help Sahiba with her good deeds. This sounds crazy. But I . . .'

'You really love this girl, don't you, bro?'

I smiled. 'I do.'

'And look, now you're blushing like a little girl!'

I think I blushed some more. Then I asked him, 'Is . . . is that even possible?'

'Bro!' he squealed. 'You're asking me if I'll allow you to help people? Of course, I would!' He waved at me. 'Come here, come here.' I moved closer to him. 'Bro, help as many people as you can. Helping is good. Maybe I'll reduce your time in purgatory then and put you straight in heaven.'

Thirty-two

'And just like that you have the power of hearing others' sufferings?'

It was early afternoon and we were sitting on Sahiba and Ginny's favourite bench in our park. The weather was mild but a little sticky. We were there for barely five minutes and I could already see beads of sweat on Sahiba's face.

She looked ahead in the distance when she asked the question. I had asked her to, for fear of people regarding her as crazy, since she would appear to be talking to herself.

'Yes,' I replied. 'Just like that. All he did was place his right palm on my chest.'

'Wow!'

'And since I wanted to do a noble thing, he gave me something extra.'

She cocked her head at me. 'Something extra?'

'No, no!' I said. 'Don't look at me! You see those people there? They'll think you have gone mad talking to yourself.'

'Okay, okay,' she said, turning away from me. 'Something extra?' she muttered.

'Yeah,' I replied, looking at her. I could do that. No one could see me. 'He said, "Apart from being able to find people who need help, you will also be able to foresee people's sufferings. I got carried away, bro, because I like you and gave you additional powers. Sahiba and you might find it useful".'

'How's that even possible?'

'I know,' I said. 'Let me try.'

I closed my eyes and tried to concentrate. It was difficult as the only image that I saw, at least for the first few moments, was that of Sahiba. Sahiba smiling. Sahiba crying. Sahiba hugging me. Her arms going through me. Sahiba laughing. Then slowly her face dematerialized and I heard a scream. I tried to focus and recognize the voice, or at least establish the location of its origin.

'I hear a scream,' I replied, my eyes still closed.

'Good, good,' she said. 'Tell me more. This can be our first.'

I concentrated harder, trying to block out all the sounds around me—the bark of a few dogs somewhere nearby, the ringing of a temple bell, a vegetable seller's sharp bellow, the soft murmur of birds above—and slowly I saw a face. Oh, it was the daughter of Mehta Aunty, I think, from C-block. But why was she screaming? A burglar, perhaps. No, she was looking at the wall in front of her. What is it? What is it? Oh, damn . . . it's a lizard.

'That Parul, I think that's her name, from C-block.' I opened my eyes.

'Why is she screaming? I'll help her.' Her eyes were sparkling now.

'It's a lizard.'

'Oh.' I saw my answer quickly flush out all the hope from her face. 'What the hell can I do with that? Go over and chase out a damn lizard?' She shook her head and looked at me. 'Harry, you got to do better than that.'

'Don't . . . don't look at me! How many times should I tell you that? Pull out your phone and speak into it.'

She did as told. She said, 'Think Harry, think! Prayers alone wouldn't help. God wants me to do these good deeds before returning Sidhu to me.'

I wanted to tell her he won't be back, but didn't. Time is the best healer. Good deeds might make her move on. So I played along, closed my eyes again, and phased out everything around me. I drew myself deeper and deeper in my mind's eye.

'What do I see . . . what, what, what . . . oh, flames billowing. Not too far from here.' I could feel Sahiba moving restlessly beside me. I looked behind my shoulder. 'There . . . A-block, my building. Third floor. Oh wait . . . that's Firdaus's floor. We used to play cricket together a few years ago. He lives with his old, nasty mother. Oh, she's crying. No, howling in pain. Firdaus, too. They've lost their house.'

'Anybody stuck in the fire?'

I closed my eyes. 'Let's see . . . no, no, nobody. I hear screams, though. Oh no, that's the mother screaming on the phone, calling . . . calling a fire brigade, I think. Flames going up the wall now. An antique watch catching fire. The needles at right angles, smaller one at three . . . the fire is getting stronger as we speak . . .'

'Wait, wait, smaller needle at three?'

I opened my eyes and said, 'Yes.' She was again looking at me and the phone was not pressed to her ear. So much for warning her!

'That's fifteen minutes later, Harry!'

'Could be night as well. Oh shit, no, no. I think it was daytime.'

Before I could say anything further, Sahiba rose and sped towards A-block. I ran after her. She called for the lift. We got in. She pressed the button for the third floor.

'Never make them feel like you know there'll be a fire fifteen minutes later,' I told her in the elevator. 'Otherwise, you'll have to answer a lot of questions.'

As we got out, to our left, Firdaus and his nasty mother stepped out of their flat. Firdaus inserted the key in the lock and turned it clockwise.

'Going somewhere, guys?' Sahiba asked, casually.

'Who are you?' the nasty mother spat.

'Mom, she lives . . .' He looked at Sahiba. 'In B-block, right?'

'Right.'

'What do you want?'

Sahiba smiled ingratiatingly. 'Actually we are working . . .'

'Who's we?'

Sahiba gave a quick glance in my direction, then shook her head. 'No, I mean I'm working for a children's NGO. We are looking for donations to help them with their education.'

She fixed Sahiba with a nasty stare. 'What's the name of the NGO?'

I could see Sahiba's lower lip tremble. 'Help . . . Help India.'

Firdaus pulled out his wallet from the back pocket of his jeans, rummaged through it and handed her a hundred-rupee note.

'Thanks.'

'You don't have a receipt or something?'

'Don't worry, Aunty. I won't steal this money. Er . . . could you give me a glass of water, if you don't mind? I've been running around since morning.'

She heaved a deep sigh and shook her head. Before she could say anything, Firdaus unlocked the door and led her inside. In the kitchen, he pulled out a glass from a cabinet, a bottle from the fridge and handed her both.

'Thanks,' she said, pouring water in the glass and looking around sneakily. 'What's that smell?'

'What smell?' Firdaus asked.

'That smell!' She sniffed a couple of times.

'What smell?' Firdaus's mother asked this time.

'Can't you smell it?' she asked both the mother and the son. 'That's . . . that's gas! Oh see, you've left the burner on!' She reached for it and turned it anti-clockwise. Then she spotted an electric kettle with the power on. 'See over there, that thing could have short-circuited and produced a tiny spark and with so much propane in the air . . . Boom!'

When we left their flat, Firdaus's mother thanked her, apologized for being nasty and then thanked her again.

'That can be my first good deed, right?' Sahiba said and winked at me in the elevator.

Thirty-three

When you truly love someone, you are always talking to yourself. Second-guessing yourself. Doubting yourself. But Yama had given me the gift of listening to other people's sufferings, not their random talks. And that's exactly what I heard.

There is a lover's spot close to our neighbourhood, just a few kilometres away. It's a small park on the outer periphery of a mall where young couples hang around. But apart from that, Sahiba told me, there were lots of lonely men and women too who visit the place. They were those who had loved and lost, and were trying to forget their past and start over, looking for fresh beginnings.

But love is not that simple, is it? It's hard. I don't think there is anyone in the world who has loved and lost, and forgotten about it with the next sunrise. Everyone has to suffer their share of pain.

So now, what I heard, were sad and painful voices. But, among them, the one that stood out was, 'One chance, one last chance, God, please, just one chance!' There was so much melancholy in the voice that everything else seemed nothing more like static on a radio.

It wasn't hard to identify the owner of the voice. A young boy, not more than Sahiba's age, was sitting to our left on the slightly wet grass and gazing sadly up at the sky. Tears . . . no, no tears. Just pain and hope in his eyes.

'That guy is very sad,' I told Sahiba, nodding towards him.

Her eyes twinkled gleefully. 'Wow!' she exclaimed.

'You're happy that he's sad? You sadist!'

'No, no,' she replied, sauntering towards him. I followed her. Looking over her shoulder, she said to me, 'He's sad and I'm happy that I can help him.'

'Hey,' she said to the boy. 'Why are you so sad?'

He looked up at her dubiously. He sniffed and ran a quick hand over his eyes. 'Excuse me?'

'I asked why you are sad.'

He ran both his hands over his shoulder-length hair. He looked like some kind of a rock star who overdoses on dope. 'Why do you care?'

'It's called humanity.'

He shook his head in exasperation. 'Please go. Just leave me alone.'

Sahiba looked over at me and I gave a thumbs-up sign.

'Can I help you?'

The boy looked up again. 'Please go. No one can help me.'

'Try me.'

He got up in a fit of rage, tightly held Sahiba's arms and jostled her. His hair flew all over his face. 'No one can help me. You get it? No one! Amyra dumped me. She dumped me because I had gone away for a year to learn music in London and, when I came back, she doesn't love me any more. All I want is another chance to speak my heart out to her. She doesn't want to meet me, doesn't take my calls. It seems I have troubled her so much that her mother warned me she would hand me over to the cops for stalking her daughter. So unless you can go over to her place and convince her to give me that chance, you can't help me!'

'Okay,' said Sahiba. 'I can do that.'

That same evening, Sahiba and I stood outside Amyra's bungalow in Greater Kailash. The chick was damn rich. A pretty girl opened the door.

'Yes?'

'Er . . .' Sahiba looked at me. 'We are . . . sorry, I am Sammy . . . Sameer's friend.'

'Oh my God!' the girl screamed. 'Now he's sending his friends over to my place! What's wrong with that psycho?'

'Amyra . . . Amyra, listen,' Sahiba said. 'I know I shouldn't be doing this but all he wants is one last chance to speak to you. Please give him that.'

'Get out!' Amyra screamed.

'The man I loved was killed in an accident ten days before our wedding. I almost died with him. Every day I wish I got one last chance to be with him, to talk to him, to properly say goodbye. I know I won't get that chance, but . . .' Big, olive-sized tears emerged from Sahiba's eyes. 'But I want Sameer to get that last chance. Everyone in love deserves their one last chance. Could you please . . . please give him that?'

Few minutes later, outside Amyra's house, I told Sahiba, 'I really wish even you had got your last chance.'

'What last chance?' she asked as she got into an autorickshaw. 'That was just an act. I don't need any last chance. I'm getting Sidhu back!'

Two days later, Sahiba got a call from Sameer thanking her.

He had got his last chance.

Thirty-four

The next sound I heard were screams. Someone wailing in pain. Dust-smeared face. Blood. A bald middle-aged man, lying on the road, face down, in a puddle. I recognized the road. It was the street just outside our building.

We rushed outside and spotted the puddle to our left, opposite the ring of shops. No one was there.

'Think, Harry, think,' Sahiba said. 'When will this happen?'

I saw him then, the bald man, walking, through my mind's eye. He wasn't entirely bald, there were some strands of hair on the sides and on the back of his head. He had curled that wispy hair and brought it to the top, perhaps to fool people into thinking that he wasn't bald. Right now his carefully arranged hair on the top of his head sat like a snake waiting to hiss.

Damn, even in my mind, I could see all of it so clearly.

He was fat and flaunted his paunch. It peeked out happily from between two buttons of his chequered shirt. I saw him walking on the street outside our building. He walked past it and was soon out of sight. Oh, what the hell! Nothing happened.

'Baldie, walking, paunch . . . what is this, Harry? How do I help him?'

'Sorry, sorry, his hairstyle distracted me.' I opened my eyes.

'Hairstyle? But you said he was bald.'

'No, no, he has some hair.'

'Okay, okay, just try again.'

There was nothing eventful in what I saw next—people walking, talking, cars passing, children running around— ordinary sights of an ordinary day. I didn't see anyone in trouble or in need of help. Baldie reappeared in my head, this time carrying groceries in his right hand, a packet of brown bread visible through the polythene bag. He walked without a care in the world, the head over his very short neck undulating as he moved.

A car came speeding through in the opposite direction from his left, the tyres hitting a puddle of water and splashing it all over him. His chequered shirt and white trousers were doused with muck and water. He grimaced, turned around and yelled, 'Bastards!' The car screeched to a halt and approached him in reverse. The window towards his side rolled down and a paan-smeared mouth spoke (I couldn't see this face clearly), 'What did you say, fatso?'

Fatso repeated what he had said, then went on to explain the meaning of the word in detail. 'You are of illegitimate birth, born out of deceit, fraud. You were not meant to be born. Maybe your biological father banged your biological mother and never saw each other again.' He paused. 'Now did you understand what I said?'

Satisfied, with a smug look on his face, Baldie continued his imperturbable walk.

Then there were kicks and howls and punches and yelps.

The snake on top of Baldie's head collapsed, conceding defeat, along with him. He lay whimpering with his face down in the puddle of water.

That was the sight I had seen earlier.

The two hefty men from the car kicked his back twice before getting back in the car and driving out.

'When will this happen?' Sahiba asked me.

'I don't know. Now, maybe.'

We glanced at the puddle of water. Tons of mosquitoes hovered over it. If we didn't do something immediately, they would be sucking plenty of Baldie's blood soon.

'Okay, but where's the man, my good deed number three?' Sahiba giggled, squinting first to her left, then her right.

'What would you do?'

'I'll figure something out.'

I saw a faint profile of the man I saw in my mind walking towards us from our right. But he was far. I could not see his paunch sticking out from the two buttons of his shirt; I couldn't see the snake on the top of his head either. When he came closer, I spotted both.

'He's our guy.'

'Okay.'

When he came near the main gate of our building, about twenty metres from the puddle, Sahiba stopped him.

'Excuse me, sir.'

'Yes?' Baldie said.

I stood to their left, looking in the distance for a speeding car.

'Er . . . what time is it?'

'You're also wearing a watch.'

'It isn't working.'

Baldie made a face, lifted Sahiba's hand and read the time from her watch. 'See, it's working.'

Clueless, she looked at me. I nodded at a car turning towards this road. That might be it.

'Sir, your hair . . . how did you manage to bring it to the top?'

'What?' he asked. 'What nonsense?'

He tried to move ahead but Sahiba got in the way. 'No, no, sir. I mean my father is also bald and I want to suggest this hairstyle to him.'

There was a splash behind us and the tyres threw water in all directions. No one was close by to get drenched. No one hurled abuses, the car didn't stop and no one got beaten up. Our job was done.

Baldie, however, was shaking his head irritably now. 'You're high, young lady!' He stormed past her. Sahiba didn't stop him this time.

'Next time, come up with a better idea,' I said, laughing. 'You want to suggest his hairstyle to your father? Come on Sahiba, you embarrassed the poor man!'

All she could do for an answer was break into peals of laughter.

Thirty-five

And so, lo and behold, two weeks passed that way during which Sahiba managed almost a dozen good deeds. She went out of her way to help people, sometimes eliciting angry, confused expressions, and at other times, messing up completely.

For instance, two days ago, in the café close to our neighbourhood, I saw a young woman fidgeting in her seat, biting her nails. She was very disappointed and heartbroken. It was her boyfriend. He had not turned up that day, like so many other times, coming up with a lame excuse for his absence. She had had enough of it. She questioned herself if he was even worth it. Unreliable bastard.

Then, I saw the Unreliable Bastard, few moments ahead in time, planning a big surprise for her. It was the anniversary of their bittersweet relationship and everyone in the café, the woman would later realize, had a souvenir for her, carefully picked by her boyfriend. These would be presented to her in a way that would remind her of every month they had spent together.

'I'll go tell her then,' said Sahiba. 'She's almost on the verge of tears, Harry. I can't see her like that.'

'It's a surprise!'

'What surprise?' Sahiba looked at the young woman. 'Oh see, there comes the tears. Aww . . . '

'You stupid girl, that's the way to do it. Lower the expectations first and then . . . bam . . . surprise!'

Sahiba couldn't resist watching her cry. She got up and walked up to her. 'Don't cry, please,' she said. 'Don't cry.'

Confused, the young woman looked up. Sahiba handed her a napkin.

'Thank you.' She wiped her eyes with it.

'Don't cry,' Sahiba said again. 'It's just a prank. He wants to surprise you.'

Five minutes later, when the Unreliable Bastard showed up at the door and everyone in the cafe screamed 'Surprise!' the young woman glared at Sahiba and hissed out one word.

Sahiba turned to me. 'What did she say, Harry? I couldn't make out. Was it thanks?'

'No,' I said. 'Not thanks.'

'Then?'

'Bitch!'

Anyway, this is a part and parcel of life. You win some, you lose some.

Almost a month after Siddharth's death, in mid-September, Sahiba stepped inside her bakery. Her family had been urging her to get back to work for the past two weeks. Other than the fact that the business was getting affected because of her absence, they believed it would be a good distraction for her and would keep her busy. Her mother and sister took care of it in her absence.

Just outside the bakery, a couple of scrawny children in tattered clothes begged, their hands rhythmically moving up towards their mouth, indicating they were hungry. Sahiba looked inside her purse, pulled out two hundred-rupee notes, and handed them one each. Their eyes lit up like powerful light bulbs. After quickly plucking it out of her hand, they moved their hands over their stomach.

'Oh, poor kids,' sighed Sahiba. 'They are so hungry.'

'They'll always be hungry, Sahiba, no matter how much you give them.'

'Shut up, Harry. Don't be so insensitive.'

She looked towards her bakery, and suddenly, a gleam of delight came on her face.

She turned to the two hungry kids. 'Do you kids like Italian food?'

'What the hell are you up to now?' I screamed and ran after her as she hopped the stairs towards her bakery.

The delicious aroma of freshly baked cakes and garlic bread took my breath away as Sahiba pushed open the glass door. She had personally trained all her bakers, who worked diligently on the other side of a glass-partitioned wall, just behind the counter where Siddharth used to sit. Now Sahiba's father sat there, printing out receipts and settling the accounts.

'Hey, Shankar Da, how is it going?'

'Good, Sahiba Didi.'

Shankar was an obsequious, overly innocent man. He was Sahiba's prime assistant. He took care of the bakery, watched over the other workers and settled the bills when no one from the family was around.

'Back to work?' Dad asked Sahiba, handing the change to a customer with a smile.

'No,' said Sahiba, irritably. 'I've so much work of my own.'

'Like bringing back a dead man?' Aashima asked. 'Come on, Sahiba . . .'

Sahiba didn't see this, but I did. Dad threw a sharp look at Aashima and she quickly changed her track.

' . . . he'll be back when he wants to be back.'

Sahiba ignored her. She looked back at her father. 'Actually, I . . . I wanted to ask you something.'

'What?'

'I don't want to make any money from this bakery,' she said, matter-of-factly. 'Sidhu helped me build this. It wouldn't be what it is without him.'

'Okay. So?'

'I want to make it a free bakery.'

Dad removed his spectacles, placed them on the desk in front of him and leaned back, confused. 'Free bakery?' He glanced at Aashima. Aashima threw her hands up in the air behind Sahiba's back. Her sister had gone mad.

'Daddy, I really believe Sidhu will come back if I complete a thousand good deeds. I speak to God every day in my prayers and He tells me that.' She looked behind her shoulder at Aashima. 'There are so many beggars here. How can I keep making money when people are dying of hunger outside?'

Daddy just smiled and slowly shook his head. 'Okay,' he said. 'Okay.'

Two hours later, there was a sign outside Angel's Basket. It read:

Free bakery. But please pay if you can.

Thirty-six

Sahiba would count her good deeds every day. Every single day.

'Only forty-eight,' she said to me in the last week of September. 'It's been forty days and I only managed forty-eight, Harry. Something's got to be done.'

'What about all the free food you're giving away in your bakery?'

She dismissed it with an irritated wave of her hand. 'Free doughnuts and pastries. Do you really think that counts? It just feels good to feed the hungry. They can't be counted as good deeds!'

'Of course they can be.'

'Okay, then,' she said, not very convinced. 'Maybe one a day. That makes it . . .' She counted on her fingers. '. . . at the most fifteen good deeds. So in all about sixty, more or less.'

'Not bad, right?'

'Not bad?' she almost screamed. Some of the people in our colony, who were out for their evening walk, craned their necks at her. Luckily, she had her phone pressed to her ear.

She looked at them sheepishly and murmured into the phone, 'Aashima, you know how she is.' They walked on.

'Not bad, Harry?' she asked again, very softly this time. 'At that speed, it'd take me about three years to complete a thousand good deeds!'

I rolled my eyes heavenwards. 'So then what's your plan?'

The next day she enrolled in two NGOs—Children's Care, which taught underprivileged kids for free and The Old Man's NGO, which helped old and disabled people.

The first was in an east Delhi neighbourhood, few kilometres from her place. She told me it was a new establishment and that the organizers were looking for more volunteers. One of them, a plump, bespectacled woman, who introduced herself as Manju, thanked Sahiba profusely and told her she was the first person who'd joined them on her own accord. They'd been making calls, urging people to come forward, but she said everybody was too busy these days to help. Sahiba told her she had all the time in the world.

She would reach the place at nine in the morning, quickly read through the course material first and then teach with the seriousness of a college professor. There were kids of all ages, some enthusiastic, some not so. While some were there to learn, others came for the morning snacks and free lunch.

She'd be free by early afternoon and would then proceed to the second NGO. Here she'd spend time interacting with the oldies, listening to their stories, helping them, assisting the administrators procure clothes, funds and more volunteers.

All in all, she said, it was a very feel-good experience.

'Why was I not doing this earlier?' she asked me one evening. I noticed the melancholy in her eyes.

As much as I enjoyed my time with her, I was filled with doubt and uncertainty. Was I really helping her or forcing her down a cliff? A thousand good deeds were good. It would no doubt make her a better person and bring her happiness, but to expect a miracle was taking it too far. To expect Sidhu would be back . . .

This fear was echoed by each of her family members, too. I eavesdropped on their conversation one Saturday night when Sahiba was asleep. But like me, they never said anything to her. They let her believe in her dream, hoping time would be the saviour.

Her mother spearheaded this conversation. The three of them sat in the master bedroom, the door firmly shut. 'What now, Ranjit?' Mom asked. 'Sahiba's belief is getting stronger.'

Aashima didn't conceal her fear as well. 'It worries me too, Mom, Dad. It's been more than a month now and I really wonder . . .'

'But she's happy,' said Dad. 'She's really happy, don't you guys see that? If a few deeds can do that, imagine what a thousand would do.'

'But it's the end objective that worries me,' said Mom.

'Yeah,' said Aashima. 'And I can't be in the bakery day in, day out. I have to complete the book I'm working on. You know that, Dad. Besides, how can a dead man come back to life?'

'I don't know.'

'Should we do something?' Big, curved lines of worry appeared on Mom's forehead.

'I don't know that either.'

The discussion went on for half an hour and Dad concluded by saying, 'I have faith in God. He'll help her.'

Thirty-seven

'I have faith in God. A lot of it. Immense faith, actually.'

This was Sahiba response when Ginny asked her, 'Do you really think He'll help you?'

It was a sunny Sunday evening in the first week of October. The rains had been paltry this year and I didn't mind it. I never liked Delhi rains. They wreak havoc in the city—waterlogging, diseases, traffic jams. Anyway, this was back when I was alive; I didn't care now.

We sat in an open-roofed café, soaking in the sun. Sahiba and Ginny sat in wicker chairs set across a round glass table. I sat on the round silver railings to Sahiba's right. She drank cappuccino and Ginny, mocha.

From across the table, Ginny squeezed Sahiba's hand. 'I like what you're doing, Sahiba. But . . . but believing that Siddharth will be back . . .'

'He will, Ginny, he will.'

Sahiba's voice was firm, unrelenting. It made me doubt my intentions again. Yama's words rang clear in my head—he's not coming back. He didn't seem to be someone who'd go back on his words. But what was the other option? Telling her Siddharth is in heaven and there is no way he's coming back because, you see, Yama, the God of Death, told me that? What would she do with that piece of information?

Tailspin into depression, of course. She'd be devastated. She'd stop what she was doing now. She'd stop believing. And I didn't want that. Hope is a good thing, even if it's unrealistic and far-fetched.

Yes, hope is good.

I made up my mind. I won't tell her anything, not until she finishes her thousand deeds. Then I'll perhaps reanalyse my options. My wish: I wanted Sahiba to be happy, Siddharth or no Siddharth. Period.

'I worry for you, sweetheart, I really do.' Ginny leaned back. Her eyes held concern and apprehension. They were small and she'd squeezed them, making them smaller still. She took a small sip and placed the plastic glass on the table in front of her. Leaning forward and crossing her arms on the table, she said, 'Are you sure someone can come back once they are gone?'

'Do you believe in miracles, Ginny?'

'Not as much as you do.'

'I believe in them. They happen all the time.'

Settling back on her chair again, Ginny said after a brief smile, 'Okay.' She thought for a while and nodded a little.

Then she apologized that she wasn't able to help her. Medicine wasn't an easy course to pursue, she told her. It entailed long hours in college, followed by assignments at home. Sometimes they did repulsive things, dissecting bodies and examining organs, and those days, she'd throw up and spend her evenings in bed.

From now on, however, she promised she'd spend at least the weekends helping her in her pursuit.

'Right then,' said Ginny. 'Let's try and make a miracle happen.'

Ginny convinced Sahiba to go with her to a south Delhi mall the following Sunday. She told her it had been ages since the two of them had spent a day together. They planned to watch a movie and go shopping, followed by dinner at Sahiba's favourite restaurant, The Italian Colony. I had nothing much to do, so I tagged along.

The weather was pleasant and after booking two seats for the evening show from the ticket counter just outside the mall, they sauntered along the huge open space behind it. Being a weekend, the place teemed with people. There were makeshift stalls sprawled along the outer periphery—little bronze showpieces on display in one of them, ethnic clothing in another, gifts and cards, toys, accessories—there were plenty to choose from. They idled for some time in the clothing stall, asked for the price of this and that, wrinkled their noses in surprising similarity and then moved on.

Ginny got coffee from a bustling café nearby and asked Sahiba about the good deeds she'd been planning for that day. Sahiba cast a furtive smile at me and said she couldn't plan them. She helped when someone needed help. Ginny said that something better could surely be arranged, one in which a lot of people could be helped.

'You have an idea?'

'Not at the moment.'

'When you have it, please, please tell me.'

Ginny said she would, most definitely. We knew, however, that she couldn't come up with a better idea than our current one.

When she walked over to the nearest dustbin to dispose of their empty coffee glasses, Sahiba asked me if I could hear anything. Is anyone sad? Does anyone need help? I told her I'd been trying, but heard nothing substantial. I could see the disappointment on her face when she nodded.

We entered the mall. A whiff of cool air suffused with a pleasant fragrance greeted us. There were more people here, young and old, friends, couples and families, all with large plastic bags in their hands, as if the shops were doling out items for free. The cafes and restaurants—there were only a few on the ground floor—appeared to be the most crowded places and loud voices poured out as we passed them.

'You want to eat something?' Ginny asked Sahiba.

Sahiba shook her head.

'Then let's shop.'

They entered the store of a woman-only brand. Sahiba looked behind her shoulder for me. I motioned her to carry on. Finding nothing much to do outside, I went into the shop after a few minutes. Ginny was persuading Sahiba to try out the dress she'd picked for her. Sahiba said she was perfunctorily looking at it; she did not intend to buy it.

'You've been through hard times lately,' said Ginny. 'Some shopping wouldn't hurt.'

Sahiba conceded, removed the dress from the hanger and walked behind us to the changing room. She emerged two minutes later, looking stunning. It was an olive-coloured dress, dropping till just above her knees, and fitted her perfectly. Ginny said the dress was beautiful and tailor-made for her, and insisted she buy it at once. Sahiba considered it, looked at me and very faintly cocked her head. I gave her a thumbs-up sign. She nodded.

A woman, who appeared to be in her early twenties, accompanied by another woman, also seemingly in her twenties, walked in. The first woman shuffled through the dresses on the stand. 'It was right here,' she said to her friend. She continued shuffling. 'And now it's not here,' she said a minute later. She turned, saw Sahiba wearing it, and frowned.

'Oh, are you buying that?' she asked Sahiba.

'She is,' said Ginny. 'Why?'

'I really liked it. I went over looking for my friend to show her . . .'

'Take it!' said Sahiba.

'No!' cried Ginny. 'Sorry,' she said to the girl who wanted it. 'She's already set her mind on buying it.'

'No, Ginny, it's okay.' She said to the girl, 'I'll just go back inside and take it off.'

'No,' said Ginny, furiously. 'You're not! You like it and you are buying it.'

'She likes it, Ginny. Let her have it.' She turned to the girl, 'Please give me a minute.'

A minute later, the girl had the dress.

Ginny walked out of the store shaking her head, Sahiba smiling beside her.

'You and your good deeds, crazy girl!'

Thirty-eight

In the evening, they went to watch an art film, one with no songs, few dialogues and long, dragging, boring scenes. The kind of movie where, at the end, you have to think really hard what the fuck it was all about. It was Ginny's idea. Both Sahiba and I exchanged bored glances from time to time. While Ginny sat glued to the screen, Sahiba yawned away the entire time.

Sometime during the movie, I heard screams. A lot of screams. And painful wails. A lot of people crying and screaming together. I shut my eyes and tried to concentrate. I tried to go back to it. The scenes started playing in reverse. Everything appeared normal, routine. Then suddenly a shudder ran through me. Oh . . . there it is. A blast! Large, consuming flames. Bodies flying in the air.

When the next set of images started forming in my mind, I realized the blast would take place somewhere inside this mall. I hurriedly told this to Sahiba; her mouth fell open and she snorted. Ginny turned to her and asked her what happened. Sahiba shook her head and told her she'd like to use the washroom.

'In the middle of the movie?' Ginny whispered.

Sahiba had already risen by then. 'Sorry, I've got a small bladder.' She stumbled her way through, disturbing those in the seats next to the aisle.

We took the exit to our right and proceeded to the women's washroom. Inside, Sahiba inspected the doors of all the cubicles and after confirming the place was empty, said, 'A blast?'

I nodded. 'I can't fill the when and where.'

'Think, Harry, think!'

I paced up and down nervously, later realizing with some embarrassment that it was a women's washroom. Two middle-aged women walked in then and looked at Sahiba suspiciously. She was standing in the middle of the room doing nothing. She unzipped her handbag hurriedly, retrieved her phone and pretended to dial a number. On the phone she said, 'When and where, Harry?'

The two women had by then proceeded to the cubicles and closed the doors behind them.

I remembered seeing a glass door smash to pieces and above it a green exit sign melting.

'It's near one of the exit doors,' I told Sahiba.

'But which one?' she asked. 'There are so many.'

'Then we'll have to check it all.'

We hurried out and took the elevator down to the ground floor. I told her to look for any suspicious objects, any unaccompanied luggage.

'But shouldn't we be informing the police?'

'I don't think there's enough time for that.'

She agreed and we ran towards the first exit door. It led to restaurants and bars on the other side of the road. Besides the exit, there was also an entry gate to this mall there, closely monitored by guards and X-ray machines. This shouldn't be the one, I thought. We scanned the entire area, nevertheless, and couldn't find anything fishy.

Next, we came to another exit but this was an entry to the adjoining mall. Since the sign was similar to the one in my vision, we thoroughly checked it. There was a narrow passageway behind the sign, adorned with full-size mirrors on both sides. It proved to be quite a distraction as I saw some women, their eyes on the mirror, colliding with the women coming from the opposite direction also engaged in self-appraisement.

'Found anything?'

Sahiba shook her head.

We rushed to the next. Even before I started looking, I knew this was it. From where I stood, I saw the exit door a little to my right, the sign above encased in a green box, the alphabets carved out in white. To the left of the door, there was a concierge standing behind a grand teak desk, dressed in formals, addressing any query directed at him. Although I didn't see this, there was a fair chance all of this could have been annihilated by the blast.

My thoughts were interrupted by Sahiba's screams into the phone. 'Where the hell are you lost, Harry?'

'Yeah, sorry.'

'I found it!' she said and looked around stealthily. Lowering her voice to a whisper, she said, 'It's there, behind the trolleys.'

I turned. 'Yeah, that could be the one. Check it!' It was a black backpack seemingly abandoned behind the trolleys, resting by the wall.

'How?'

I shrugged.

She swallowed and I heard a small click in the back of her throat. Then a slight nod. She moved behind towards the trolleys and pulled one out. Then a charade of not liking the trolley. She chose another one. She pulled out two more until the bag was clear of the obstruction.

'All these trolleys are defective, their wheels don't move!' she cried.

The concierge politely excused himself from the customer he was speaking to and walked up to her. He adjusted his tie.

'What's the problem, ma'am?'

'Hey, whose bag is that?' asked Sahiba to the concierge.

He looked at it, narrowing his eyes. Then shaking his head, he proceeded towards it cautiously.

'Don't let him touch it,' I said. 'A slight motion could trigger it.'

The concierge bent down.

'Don't!' she warned, when he held out his arm to touch the bag. 'What if it's a bomb?'

A dozen or so people had crowded behind them, some nervous, some frightened, others nonchalant.

'No, ma'am, it wouldn't be. It's a safe mall.' But even as he said it, he realized the falsity of his own words and pulled back. 'Prudence never hurts, does it?' He pulled out his phone from the side pocket of his dark blazer and dialled a number.

Ten minutes later, the bomb squad took control of the place. Yellow-and-black striped tape secluded the area. Inside this, in protective coveralls and face shields, two men proceeded cautiously towards the bag. Outside it, despite the shoving and pushing of angry police officers, a ring of crowd stood watching. Media persons crowded outside the exit door with their flashy cameras and microphones, all speaking at once, giving their own assessment and conclusion. Terrorist organizations ISIS and LeT were mentioned copiously while others declared it an act of internal conflict.

The two brave men managed to diffuse the bomb and any casualty or damage was avoided. There was a long and loud applause from the crowd; the media gathered and began firing their questions at whoever was willing to answer. Before Sahiba could be the centre of attention, I led her away from the crowd.

After the entire ruckus, we took our seats in the theatre and seeing Ginny's concentration, Sahiba deferred the news of the bomb. When we exited the theatre, she asked her, 'Do you even know what happened today?'

'What?'

Sahiba told her everything, leaving aside the truth about me, of course.

Ginny stared at her friend, the palm of her right hand flying to her chest as if to calm down the heart that would burst out. 'Oh my God, Sahiba,' she cried, uproariously. 'You saved so many lives! That's more than a hundred good deeds put together!'

Thirty-nine

The next thing Sahiba did was extremely rash and avoidable.

During dinner, the imprudent girl told Ginny about me. That she sees me. A ghost.

Ginny had just taken a huge sip of iced tea when Sahiba said, 'Ginny, I don't want to hide this from you any more. I see Harry's ghost.'

Ginny spat out the entire contents of her mouth on to Sahiba's face. Good. She deserved it.

'Sorry, sorry,' said Ginny. 'Oh, I'm so sorry. It has spilled onto your T-shirt as well. Go wash it. It'll get stained otherwise.' She took another sip. 'Wait, what?' This time she swallowed the tea. 'You see Harry's ghost? Harry . . . that . . . that Harvinder whose tongue used to hang out like a dog whenever he saw you . . .'

'My tongue never used to hang out like a dog whenever I saw you,' I told Sahiba, embarrassed beyond measure.

'. . . that Harry who used to always snoop around behind us?'

'You knew about my favourite hobby?'

'We were not stupid, Harry!' Sahiba laughed, wiping her tee with a paper napkin and some water.

'. . . that Harry who would . . . '

'Can you please tell her to stop, Sahiba?'

'Okay, stop, stop, Ginny,' Sahiba continued laughing, one hand over her stomach and the other stretched out. 'I think you got it.'

'He's dead?'

'Yes, he died five years ago.'

Ginny swallowed the huge lump I saw form in her throat. It was as if her throat was transparent. She gulped down another sip of the iced tea.

'And you . . . you see his ghost?'

Sahiba nodded.

Ginny thumped the plastic glass on the table. 'Are you going crazy? Is he . . . is he here now?'

'Yes, he is sitting on this chair. Oh wait, now he's . . . okay, now he's sitting on your lap.'

Ginny pulled back and inspected her surroundings. I was looking right into her eyes. 'He's . . . he's sitting on my lap? I . . . I . . .' She tried again. 'I don't see him. Why do I not see him?'

'Because he's here for me. To help me carry out my good deeds.'

I got out of Ginny's lap. 'Why did you have to say that to her?'

'Because she's my friend.'

So over the next fifteen minutes or so, she told her everything about me—how I help her with the good deeds, how I have the power to look into the future and see people's sufferings, about Yama, Chitragupta, everything. As if she would believe her!

'What do you have to say about that, Ginny?'

'I thought all of this happens only in movies and books!' Ginny squealed. 'My God, this is so incredible!'

'Penne pasta for you ma'am and a thin-crust vegetable pizza for you,' said the waiter, placing the plates on the table as Ginny continued, looking at Sahiba in awe.

~

'My God,' squeaked Akshara. 'She believed her?'

I nodded. 'It surprised me a lot, but yeah, she did.' Akshara looked at me in disbelief.

'Wait . . . wait, did I not tell you not to disturb me until I complete the story? You distract me, Akshara.'

'I'm sorry, Harry. It's just that . . . just that, you know, she's such a great friend! She reminds me of Mishi, my best friend. Even she trusts me, never doubts me like everyone else does.'

'Good for you, kiddo. It's good to have nice friends.' I paused. 'Can I proceed now?'

Akshara put a finger to her lips and nodded vigorously.

Forty

Over the next three months or so, Sahiba remained fairly optimistic of Siddharth's return. She firmly believed that when the number of good deeds crosses thousand, Siddharth would magically reappear. But how? She didn't have an answer to that.

Her family, Ginny and I continued supporting and encouraging her, playing along, telling her that we believed her. Aashima didn't want to do this any more; she thought it was stupid. Her father, however, convinced her to.

'Some more time,' he'd say to his wife and elder daughter. 'I'm sure she'll be all right.'

Her mother had a very bad feeling about this. She constantly fretted that this would have a rebound effect, that after a few months, when nothing would happen, her daughter would tailspin into depression.

Personally, I wondered every day if we should continue with this charade. None of them knew it better than me that Siddharth was not coming back. But I did nothing, and the reason for my inaction was Sahiba's happiness. She had a purpose to live now and that is all one needed. I kept telling her about the sufferings of people I saw and heard around me and she did her best to avert them, as if they were her own.

There were days, however, when she realized the absurdness in what she tried to do. I remember the first time she asked me this question was in December, just a few days before New Year. Her family was out for a wedding. She had feigned a headache as she wanted to talk to me.

'Do you think I'm stupid, Harry?'

We were sitting in the balcony of her apartment—a small, semi-circular extension of the flat. Dusk was setting in and it was beginning to get chilly.

'Why do you ask that?'

She pinched her lips. Her eyes were moist. 'Will he really come back? Sometimes I think all this will be for nothing.'

Maybe, I thought, it was time to tell her what I knew. 'What do you think?' I asked instead.

She didn't wipe the tears that had rolled down her cheeks. 'I think God will not turn a deaf ear to my prayers. He'll bring Sidhu back. I trust Him.'

I raised my arms. 'There you go.' Her tears stopped me from telling her the truth. Tell her what Yama said. I decided I would do it some other time, perhaps when she wasn't crying.

'But how will He do this?' she asked, worried. 'He's dead!'

Then there were days when she was cheerfully optimistic about Siddharth's return. Two weeks later, I asked her the same question, 'How will He do this?'

And she said, 'Harry, come on. He's God. He'll have a thousand ways to do this.'

I think the overly optimistic people are a little delusional. They keep feeding lies to themselves consciously till they truly begin to believe that it is the truth. Of course, Sahiba knew there would be no miracle, but she continued to believe otherwise, nevertheless.

That was not a problem as long as she managed to get through her life. There were days, however, when his loss would torment her. This phase began from January 2013 onwards. She would be fine on most days, happily working with NGOs, listening to what I told her, offering a helping hand wherever required and always asking me at the end of the day what the final tally of her good deeds was. But sometimes she would howl in pain.

It could be a sudden trigger—watching a couple from a distance, remembering a conversation with Siddharth while talking to me or just simply feeling low. The wails would suddenly erupt out of her, like an explosive release of suppressed emotions. She would think about the lies she'd been feeding herself about the return of Siddharth and the loss, and I would hate God at that time so much for taking her love away. I'd feel like meeting Yama and requesting, pleading and begging him to change his mind. But I know, he wouldn't.

The tip of her nose would become a deep red colour and the skin below her eyes baggy. She'd skip her meals that day and pray to God the entire evening. Aashima, Ginny or her mother would try consoling her, begging her to move on.

'Why move on?' she would scream, teary-eyed. 'He is coming back! I don't care how God does it, but He's giving me my Sidhu back!'

One evening in February, almost six months after Siddharth's death, Sahiba and I were walking through our neighbourhood. She inserted the earpieces of her phone into her ears, pretending to be on a call. I spotted a couple of parrots, the colour of their beaks as deep as that of a cherry atop a tree nearby. Few squirrels darted to our left, tinkling on the fallen leaves. Shrills of kids playing and running filled the air.

She told me that she had decided to do the good deeds even after Siddharth returned.

'I never knew helping others could feel so good.'

'That's very nice of you, Sahiba.'

'There's another thing I have decided,' she continued. 'Since keeping a count of the good deeds is an intractable proposition, I've decided to do away with the counting.'

'But how would you know?'

'Let God keep a count,' she said, cheerfully. 'And when satisfied, let Him give back Siddharth.'

Forty-one

There is no rationale for love. Sahiba exemplified this. She read somewhere that a human body has ten pints of blood, fifteen per cent of which can easily be donated without any repercussions.

Besides working for NGOs—she had joined a lot more after the first two—she started visiting blood banks frequently to donate blood. She would insist on donating more than the allowed limit. Others needed it more than her, she would say, and it might help to save someone's life instead of just flowing in her veins.

Ha!

The nurses would literally throw her out, asking her to produce some blood first, before returning to donate more. But she would rejoin the queue soon after making one donation, pressing the bandage on her arm tight.

Crazy girl, Sahiba!

She had also signed up to donate her eyes, kidneys, heart, lungs, liver—any organ that can be transplanted—after death.

I wouldn't have been surprised if she would have donated them right away, had there been an option!

'Some more good deeds, no?' she'd then ask me.

It was August. On the tenth of the month, on Siddharth's death anniversary, Sahiba spent the entire day crying. And praying. She locked herself in the room and no one was allowed in. Not even me. Normally, she prayed for two hours, twice a day. But she prayed for six hours that day.

Mom was in the kitchen preparing dinner. She was chopping onions. Tears flowed unhindered from her eyes. I don't know if it was due to the onions or her concern for Sahiba. Probably the latter.

Suddenly, she wheeled around on her heels.

'Have you decided now?' she asked her husband, who sat flipping through the paper disinterestedly on the dining table. He looked at Aashima.

'It's getting too much now, Dad,' said Aashima, sitting by his side. 'It's been a year now. Shouldn't we do something?'

'Guess your wait and watch is not working any more,' said Mom, throwing the onions in the pan, then ducking as some oil splashed out of it.

Dad shook his head. 'By now she would have completed her thousand good deeds, no?'

'Yeah, must have!' squealed Aashima. 'What else has she been doing since the last year?'

'Something's got to be done now,' said Mom.

Dad nodded. 'Yeah, something's got to be done.'

~

'Can I ask you a question, Harry?'

'You can ask as many questions as you want.'

Sahiba's room was warm and cosy. She'd pulled a blanket over her legs and I sat to her side. Earlier, she had responded to the call made by her mother for dinner. The four of them had sat around the table and had their meals quietly. Zibby sat by Sahiba's chair, nudging her leg. Even he looked worried. From time to time, he would pass her a blank look. The others, too, kept gazing at her in apprehension, but she lowered her eyes and calmly ate her dinner, as if all was well with the world.

Sometimes, I empathized with the rest of the family more than I did with Sahiba. Siddharth was gone and Sahiba had her year of mourning. A one-time affair. Her family members, however, saw her dying every day. I could tell Mom had lost at least ten kilograms over the last year just by watching her daughter suffer. Aashima was always sad and frustrated. She wasn't writing any more or seeing any guys. I saw her mostly at home or at the bakery shouting at the workers. And Dad never smiled. He always had a faraway look in his eyes, of hope and worry.

'Why are you with me in this?' Sahiba asked.

'What do you mean?'

'I mean you were in love with me, weren't you? And I'm sure you never liked Siddharth. So why would you want him to return?'

After a long time, the name 'Ugly Nails' came to my mind. I smiled. Sahiba wondered what that was about. 'To answer your first question,' I began. 'Honestly . . . I still love you. Always have. Always will. That's why I'm helping you.'

Sahiba smiled and blushed a little. It felt good saying that. I think it always feels good to express your love to someone.

'And secondly, you are right, I never liked him. Why would I? He scooped away my first and last love. However, as you know, he really was a great guy. You remember those times when he would ask you to spend time with me? I always thought he was mocking me. But he wasn't. He genuinely didn't want me to feel bad and, for that, I'll always respect him.'

Sahiba leaned forward and tried to squeeze my hand, but it went through. 'Thank you, Harry.'

I wanted to tell her then that I had hit him with the car the first time, and I'm very, very sorry for that. But I couldn't muster the courage and I let the sleeping dogs lie.

The very next moment, Sahiba broke down. 'You know . . .' She tried to speak but choked on her tears. 'You know why I love him so much?' she asked. Her voice was coarse and dry, evoking pity. She didn't let me answer. 'Because he was the nicest person I ever knew. And he . . . he loved me so much. Mom tells me to forget him, but how can I do that? She tells me that I have to do it someday.' She shook her head, wiping away her tears. 'I can't. I can never forget him. And you know what? I don't even have to. Wherever he is, he is watching over me, testing me, planning his return. Because . . . because, I know, even he cannot live without me.'

'Sahiba, it's . . . it's been a year now.'

'I know, I know!' she cut me like lightning—sharp and sudden. 'He'll be back, I'm telling you.' She stopped crying, wiped away the tears and suddenly there was an unyielding determination in her eyes. 'He'll be back.'

Forty-two

A few days later, Sahiba began having strange thoughts. She did an 'analysis of her life', as she liked to call it. Apparently, before Siddharth's death, she had never helped anyone, nor had she done any good deeds. So in order to make her a better person, God took him away from her.

And, of course, He would return him to her when He is sure that she has become a better person.

'Are you out of your mind?' Ginny spat. 'What is happening to you? How can you think such imbecile things?'

'I'm telling you, Ginny, that's what it is.'

Ginny shook her head in frustration.

But Sahiba truly believed this. She had told this to me as well a couple of times earlier in the week.

'Don't you see this, Ginny? I was so selfish, so self-centred, don't you remember? I had told Sidhu to give up his dream of acting and settling in Mumbai because I wanted him to help build my bakery. And he just . . . he just agreed without even saying anything . . .'

That did it. That was the sudden trigger I spoke about earlier.

She screamed while sobbing in pain, in agony. People around us turned and passed sympathetic looks. Everyone in our neighbourhood knew her story. Everyone wished no one had to endure her pain. The concerned aunties and uncles of our neighbourhood suggested many times to Mom and Dad that perhaps she needed medical help now. She wouldn't move on. She didn't want to.

That day, Ginny cried along with her, hugging her and caressing her back. 'I'm so sorry, baby. I'm so, so sorry.'

'Why, Ginny?' Sahiba withdrew from Ginny's embrace, her face awash with tears. 'Why doesn't God give me Sidhu back? It is so easy for him to perform a miracle, right? I'm doing what he asked me to do, am I not? I can't live without Sidhu!'

Ginny ran her hand across her eyes, then wiped Sahiba's tears. 'Please . . . please, Sahiba. Maybe . . . maybe you should try and . . .'

'I'm telling you, Ginny, God did this to teach me a lesson. But I learnt the lesson, don't you think? I'm not selfish any more.'

Ginny didn't reply. She moved away from her and looked ahead blankly. Tears continued to drip down her eyes. She looked to the other side to hide her tears from Sahiba and quickly wiped her tears. Beside her, Sahiba gave a sudden snort and broke down again. She lowered her head and covered her face with both hands, her sobs now sounding muffled.

'Sidhu was such a nice guy,' she said. 'He . . .' She found it hard to speak. She lifted her head. Snot dripped down her nose. 'He changed me completely. I was such a loser earlier. I lacked self-confidence and self-respect. He gave me all of that. He gave me a dream I never knew I had.' A sudden snort again. She began sobbing uncontrollably now, drawing in short, sudden breaths. Her entire body shook as though she were having a fit. Ginny came closer and hugged her. 'I . . . I never had the confidence to open a bakery, you know. Sidhu told me I could . . . I could do it. He did it by sacrificing his own dream . . .'

'It's okay, it's okay, baby,' Ginny said, patting her back.

'I love him, Ginny. I love him so much.'

'It's all right, sweetheart, it's all right.'

Sahiba withdrew from Ginny's embrace. Her cheeks were glazed with tears, eyes red and swollen, hair messy. 'I'll kill myself, Ginny. I swear I'll kill myself if Sidhu doesn't come back.'

~

Her last line to Ginny ruffled the entire family. Ginny also went on to tell them about me. That ruffled them more. Dad paced across the living room, taking short, hurried breaths. Aashima sat on the couch, legs drawn up to her chest, biting her nails. And Mom, she cried just like Sahiba did in the afternoon. Now Ginny was consoling her. Sahiba was asleep in her room.

'That's it!' Dad swore. 'I'm taking her to a psychiatrist tomorrow.'

'But how will you convince her, Dad?'

He didn't reply.

The next morning at breakfast, Dad broached the topic. Sahiba just fiddled with her spoon, moving it in circles in her cereal bowl.

'Sahiba, will you do something for me?' Dad asked.

Mom and Aashima looked on as Sahiba continued to move her spoon in circles.

'Sahiba?'

There was no response from her.

'Sahiba!' Aashima screamed.

She jerked out of her trance. 'Yeah, yeah.'

'Daddy is asking you something, *beta*,' Mom said.

'Yes, yes, Daddy?'

Dad gave a close-lipped smile. Sahiba smiled back wanly. She tucked her hair behind her ears. Her eyes looked as if someone had doused them with plenty of red syrupy liquid. They clearly looked deprived of a good night's sleep too.

'Would you do something for me?'

'Sure, Daddy.'

Before asking her, he took a spoonful of poha from the bowl on to his plate. He too moved his spoon languidly over it. He changed his mind and put the spoon back on the plate without taking a bite. 'I would like to take you to a psychiatrist, Sahiba.'

'No, Dad, please. We've had this conversation earlier.'

'Six months ago!' Dad protested. 'And I agreed. But now it's been a year. You've had your year of grieving, Sahiba. We all thought of giving you time. Mourning is also part of healing, after all. But now it's . . .'

'Please, Sahiba,' Mom intervened. 'We've supported you. We know it's been a very rough year, but . . . but you got to . . .' She shook her head. 'We made your bakery a free one because you asked us to. All of us still work there and take care of it. Dad is losing money, you know, to keep the place running.'

'Okay,' said Sahiba. 'Okay. But I'm not crazy.'

'Nobody said you are,' Dad said. 'Tomorrow then.'

Forty-three

The following afternoon, we all sat in the waiting area of south Delhi's purportedly best psychiatrist Dr Priya Menon's clinic. I didn't know why I was there, but Sahiba had asked me to come. And like always, I couldn't say no to her.

When our turn came, we descended the few steps to her office. Certificates and laurels adorned the walls. The doctor was a wispy little woman. She smiled benignly.

'Tell me,' she said, leaning forward. 'What's the problem?'

Sahiba's mother recounted the problem; Sahiba kept asserting there wasn't one.

Priya Menon nodded ominously after both of them finished talking. She looked at each one of us (not me, of course; I was standing next to her closely examining her hair and wondering if it was a wig). Aashima sat to the extreme left, then Ginny, Dad, Mom and finally Sahiba.

'I get it, Sahiba,' she began slowly. 'That you love Siddharth and want him back. Please tell me, sweetheart, how does a dead man come back to life?'

Sahiba raised her hands in disdain. 'Don't you guys believe in miracles? They happen all the time!' Her mother patted her back. She calmed down. 'I trust God, okay? I have a lot of faith in Him.'

'Honey, it's good to be positive but these things don't happen in real life.'

'Do you know there is someone playing with your hair as we speak, honey?'

Honey recoiled and swivelled her head around. 'Who's there?'

'My friend, Harry.'

She looked at Sahiba's parents. 'See? She imagines things.'

'I don't imagine things!' Sahiba yelled.

'Okay, okay, Sahiba, you don't imagine things,' said Honey, cautiously. 'So you mean this Harry, I mean the ghost of Harry, helps you do good deeds by listening to the sufferings of people around him, right?'

'Yes.' Sahiba nodded.

'Don't you think perhaps that he's not helping you at all? I mean, that you're doing all the good deeds yourself and that you're just imagining some of them?'

'What nonsense? I . . .'

'Think about it,' Honey continued. 'That first good deed of yours—how did you know there was going to be a fire in that house? You imagined it!'

'No!' Sahiba said. 'The burner was on and . . .'

'Did anyone else apart from you see that the burner was on?'

'Of course . . .'

'No one! I'm sure. Your second good deed—Harry did not tell you that boy was sad. You saw him! And then you helped him.'

I felt like taking off Honey's wig. The bitch was confusing her.

'Your third good deed—you saved that bald man from getting beaten up. Really? How did you know he would get beaten up?' When Sahiba didn't answer, Honey said, 'You imagined it!'

'Are you crazy?' Sahiba yelled. 'You mean Harry doesn't exist?'

Honey rested her arms on the desk and crossed them. She looked at Sahiba's parents, then at her. 'I think Harry exists, but only in your mind.'

Sahiba got up, the chair behind her falling with a loud thud. She threw the middle finger of her right hand at Honey and bolted out of the room, up the stairs.

'But maybe he really exists,' Ginny said, leaning forward. 'I've really seen her talking to Harry.'

'Have you seen Harry?'

'No, but . . .'

'You are her friend,' said Honey. 'You shouldn't reinforce her hallucination.' Before Ginny could rebut, Honey said to an anxious-looking Mom, 'I need to start my sessions with her. Can you get her back?'

'I'll try,' Aashima said and got up. She returned a few moments later. 'She's screaming, saying she wants to go home and doesn't want to see anybody.'

'But what about the bomb that she helped diffuse in the mall?' said Ginny.

'I don't know,' said Honey, shaking her head. 'Coincidence, maybe? Or perhaps with all her prayers over the last year and depression, she can hear the sufferings of people around her and see the future. I can't be certain now unless I start meeting her regularly.'

'How's that even possible?' Dad asked, squinting his eyes.

'I don't know. Some people are born with powers. Some inherit it during their lifetime.'

'So you're saying Harry doesn't exist?' Ginny asked in disbelief.

Honey nodded. 'I don't think he does.'

~

'What? You don't exist? But Harry, you're sitting right in front of me, talking to me. I can see you!'

'Of course you can, Akshara,' I said. 'And of course, I exist. I told you right, these people with their fancy degrees think that they know everything. They think they are gods.'

Akshara threw a confused glance at me.

'Believe me, Akshara,' I said. 'I really helped her with her good deeds. It was I who could hear the sufferings of people, not her.'

She continued to stare at me. Although it was dark, I could see the confusion on her face. All the lights in the park had come on, some yellow, some white, some flickering, others dead. The moon, watching us from above, threw a white halo around us.

She shook her head. 'No, Harry, of course I believe you. But I was just thinking that Doctor Aunty also says the same thing about me—that I imagine things.'

'Fancy degrees. They think they know everything. They think they are gods. I told you.'

'You know, sometimes I hear Mummy's voice. I don't see her, but I hear her. I told this to Daddy. Instead of trusting me, he took me to Doctor Aunty. Even she says I imagine things. See this.' She pulled out the medicine bottle from the pocket of her blue capris. 'She gave me these medicines and told me that it'll make me "normal" again. But I am normal. I don't want these medicines. I just want to see my mummy again.'

Her lips twitched. Down came the tears in a flurry. 'I want my mummy back, Harry. Not just her voice. I want her back.'

Forty-four

Another year passed. Nothing changed. Whatever that stupid psychiatrist said, Sahiba had no qualms about my existence. Thank God.

And so, I continued helping her, showing her the way. It's hard to keep track of the good deeds we accomplished because they were a lot. Sahiba said we didn't need to. God was keeping a count.

There were some more defunct love stories we rekindled, like that of the sad boy in the park. Come to think of it, there were lots of boys and girls who had lost their love, got their hearts broken and had their lives thrown into disarray. If there was a way to help them get back their loved ones, Sahiba would have done it. She had become extremely good in persuading people, and when she narrated her story, hearts would melt.

It was so disheartening to see people who were in love with each other on their separate paths. Depressed and heartbroken, but doing nothing to get their love back. And here we were—Sahiba and I. Both madly in love, ready to move the world, yet we could never have our love. Sad, depressing really.

If two people loved each other, they should be together, right? Ego, misunderstandings and miscommunication can ruin what could otherwise be extraordinary love stories. Sahiba would talk to these people.

'Love is all that there is,' she would say, sobbing softly. 'What else is there?'

She would always use her example. An extraordinary love story wasted. She was still trying, she would tell them.

And people changed. Ready to give their love another shot. The last chances are always the best ones. Often, they would work. It would make Sahiba extremely happy. She would cry. Tears of joy, followed by tears of sadness. She would crumple like a ball in her bed, knees all the way to her chest, and spend the entire night weeping.

Over the last year, whenever her parents told her to meet the psychiatrist again, she told them that it was perhaps she, Honey, who needed a psychiatrist.

'Harry doesn't exist? What is wrong with her?'

They suggested a different doctor. One in the family. Dad's cousin.

'You want the entire Sethi family to think I'm crazy?'

Her parents had no answer. Every two or three months though, they would try to persuade her again.

~

This year Aashima met her Mr Right. A bright, handsome man. They'd been in a relationship for more than six months and she wanted to tie the knot with him. Her parents wanted Sahiba too to find someone like him, to move on.

'You are just twenty-four, Sahiba,' her father and mother would tell her. 'You'll find love again.'

'I don't need to.'

'Besides I'm too old to love again,' she would add.

'You are just twenty-four!' Aashima would say and shake her head. She had found her guy at the age of twenty-eight.

As much as she could, Sahiba would try to avoid a conversation heading in that direction. She truly believed that you loved only once. What could I say to that? Even I had loved just once. Ginny thought otherwise.

'People fall in love all the time, Sahiba,' Ginny would say with conviction, as if she were talking from experience. She had none. 'Besides, love doesn't age with us. It remains fresh and radiant whatever age we find it in.'

Sahiba would just wave a hand at that.

To say that Sahiba's parents were worried would be an understatement. They were plagued and devastated. The once younger-looking Mom began looking ten years more than her age. There was no energy, no excitement left in their lives. Their meals would be scanty. They never went out. Hardly met anyone. All their conversations and thoughts revolved around Sahiba. How would she get on with her life? This was not a normal way to live one's life, they would tell her.

They were right; all she did was offer her prayers, work for NGOs and do her good deeds, with or without my help.

The little money earned through the bakery—some customers were kind enough to pay despite the 'free' tag—was further distributed amongst the poor. The bakery had become the talking point of the neighbourhood. The local media and newspapers covered it. Sahiba utilized the publicity it got. She set up a donation website. Every penny collected was further used to serve the poor.

She even thought of setting up her own NGO, one that would work on reducing the poverty levels in Delhi. She waited for some more money to pour in. The other good deeds, meanwhile, went on.

But, of course, Siddharth didn't return.

~

'I have to tell you something, Sahiba.' Enough was enough. I had finally mustered the strength to tell her that Siddharth won't return. Yama had told me that. And when the God of Death tells you that, you got to believe him.

She was washing dishes with pleasure, unlike other volunteers who made a face, frowning every now and then. During weekends, she worked in a blind school. She'd accumulate the earnings from the bakery and pass it on to the administrators of the school, urging them to ensure their kids had a sumptuous meal during weekends. There were easily more than five hundred kids studying and living in this crumpling compound behind the busiest shopping street of south Delhi. A Parsi couple had started the school almost a decade ago, when their only son had turned blind after an accident.

After the meal, Sahiba would distribute doughnuts from her bakery to the students. Then, along with the other volunteers, she would collect the empty plates, wash and set them along with the bowls, spoons and glasses on the long dining table for the next batch of students.

Mrs Khambatta, one of the administrators—a tall, bespectacled woman—had once remarked to her peers, 'What a remarkable girl she is. May God fulfil her every wish.' She didn't know Sahiba's story. God, of course, won't be able to do that.

'I'm listening,' said Sahiba, softly, making sure no one around her heard her.

When she saw me hesitating, she rolled her eyes. 'What is it, Harry?'

'Okay, Sahiba, I'm going to give this to you straight.' I closed my eyes, opened them two seconds later and said, 'Siddharth is not coming back. He never will.'

She behaved as if she didn't hear me and remained calm and nonchalant. She carefully wiped the plate with a towel and placed it to her left. She picked up another one and began scrubbing it.

'What?' I asked. 'Did you hear me?'

'Of course, he's coming back.'

'No, he's not.' And then I told her about Yama.

She took a deep breath and sighed. Then she picked up the towel, wiped her hands and pulled out her phone from the pocket of her jeans.

'He'll change his mind,' she said on the phone.

'No, he won't.'

'Yes, he would.'

She looked below, at her feet, and when she looked back up at me, she was crying. 'He will, Harry. He has to.'

'There is no easier way to say this, Sahiba—but you have to move on.'

She shook her head and removed the dirty apron from around her waist. Then she ran outside to the corridor. I followed her. From the first floor, she looked at the children playing in the muddy playground below. It was hard to tell from here if they were blind. But they were. Just like her. Unable to see the reality.

God knows that I would have done anything, had it been in my hands, to get Siddharth back. Even if it meant dying again. But . . .

'Would you do something for me?' Sahiba interrupted my thoughts. Her eyes were wet and her cheeks moist. My heart sank looking at her. 'Please?'

'Of course, of course, Sahiba.'

'Please request Yama one more time.'

'I already did, Sahiba. So many times. He . . .'

'Please, one last time.'

I nodded. 'Okay.'

'And listen,' she said. 'Tell him that if he can't give back my Sidhu, then take me where he is. You tell him that, okay?'

Forty-five

'Bro! Bro!' Yama screamed in delight when I landed in his quarters. 'Long time no see!'

I walked up to him. 'Yeah, it's been two years.'

Chitragupta stood behind him, watching attentively at the computer screen as Yama ran his fingers over it. A discussion on taking someone's life, that would lead to the creation of more Sahibas, it seems, was in progress.

As I reached his desk and glanced at the screen, I was shocked. He . . . he was playing a stupid car racing game! His fingers moved carelessly on the screen and every few seconds, his car would crash. He would grunt and then start over again.

'You can do it, my Lord! You can do it,' said Chitragupta, encouraging him. 'Little bit, just a bit more careful, my Lord.'

When his car crashed again, my Lord looked behind his shoulder and said haughtily, 'What more careful, Chitragupta? You can't even go beyond the first hurdle!'

Chitragupta's face shrank. He looked at me and said dryly, 'Hey dude.'

'Hey.'

Yama continued, starting over, and crashing every ten seconds.

'Damn!' he said, irritated after a few more crashes. 'It's been six months! I just can't clear this level.'

'Bro, that's level one!' I said. 'You can't even clear the first level? Even a five-year-old would do that in the first attempt.'

He looked at me, his brows raised in surprise. 'Really?' He thought about it and then asked, 'Could you . . . er . . . could you show me how it's done?'

I shook my head. 'I've got more important things to discuss, bro, than this stupid car racing game I used to play ten years ago!'

Yama frowned. 'That was rude, bro! Why are you so sad?'

'Because Sahiba is sad,' I replied.

Yama tried to make a sympathetic face but failed at it. 'Oh, it's that Ugl . . . Siddharth again.' It was clear from his expression that he wouldn't change his mind. He threw an arm around me like a close buddy who was going to talk of a cricket match I missed. I knew what he would say.

'I'm sorry,' said Yama.

I removed his arm from around my shoulder. 'You are a bad bro, bro.'

'How can I help you in this? I told you earlier that it's against the rules.'

'But at least . . .'

'Shh . . . shh.' He put a finger to his lips. 'Oh my God!'

'What happened?'

Suddenly an enormous gust of wind began to fill the room with an overpowering sound. Yama straightened up, adjusted his dress and raked an arm through his hair. Chitragupta did the same behind us.

'What happened? Why are you suddenly so nervous?' I asked him.

'God!'

'Yes bro, what happened?'

He wheeled around to face me, the anxiety in his eyes palpable. 'It's God. He's here!'

'What?'

After a few moments, there was a blinding white light ahead of us, its radiance illuminating the entire room. The light pierced through the smoke in the room, making it appear like white candy. The gust of wind reduced to a strong breeze and finally petered out.

Yama and Chitragupta had a look of awe on their face, along with an ingratiating smile. They brought their hands out in front and folded them in reverence, their heads bent slightly. Yama nudged me, indicating to do the same. I couldn't believe this—the white light was God?

'What . . . what brings you here, my dear Lord?' Yama asked, with his eyes downcast. 'You could have summoned me.'

God said, 'There is this girl below. She's been praying so much—so much to bring someone back.' The sound boomed through the entire room as if it was played on a high-wattage loudspeaker.

'Yes, my dear Lord,' replied Yama. 'That's Sahiba.' He turned to me. 'This is her friend, bro . . . oh sorry, Harry.'

I raised my hand. 'Hello br . . . sir.' Yama gave me a sidelong scowl.

'Do what you have to, Yamaraj. Get the girl what she wants.' After saying that, the white light began to disappear.

I was flabbergasted. That's it? Really? Sahiba would get Siddharth back?

'My . . . my dear Lord,' stuttered Yama. 'How's that even possible? The person she wants is dead. You know I can't bring him back. It's against the rules.'

'Yama,' said the white light. 'I cannot turn my back on people who have unflinching faith in me. Just do it!'

And the white light was gone.

For the next five minutes or so, Yama couldn't shake off what had just happened. Me too. Sahiba will soon get Siddharth back! Mr Ugly Nails would be back! That'd be great!

'This is not possible!' Yama shook his head. 'How do I make that happen?'

'Was that really God?'

Yama appeared startled. 'What do you mean, bro? Of course that was God.'

'No . . . no, I mean I thought God would look like a person, wear old-fashioned clothes and have more than one pair of hands. I'm talking about the Hindu God. Muslim and Christian gods would look different, of course. Back on earth, we have so many gods.'

'Oh really?' Yama asked, confused. 'That's so weird. Up here, that's the only one!'

'Uh . . . huh?'

Yama shook his head and looked behind his shoulder. 'What do we do now, Chitragupta?'

Chitragupta still had his hands folded and his head was bent. 'Whatever you say, my Lord.'

'You have any idea?'

'Actually, there's one thing we can do.'

'What?'

'You know . . . that thing.'

'What that thing?'

'That thing!'

'Oh, that thing!' Yama said with relief. 'Yeah, of course. How could I forget? Sure, we can do that thing!'

Forty-six

'What thing, Harry?' Akshara asked, bubbling with excitement. 'Does that . . . does that mean Sahiba Didi gets Sidhu Uncle back?'

I nodded. 'She does.'

Akshara's hands flew to her gaping mouth. 'Really?' She moved closer to me. 'Really, Harry? How? How?'

'You remember, before I started narrating this story, you told me you read somewhere that when you always think of a loved one who has died, miss them and cry for them, they return as your guardian angel and are always with you?'

'Oh my God! So that was true? Sidhu Uncle becomes Sahiba Didi's guardian angel?'

I nodded again.

'That is so great, Harry! So how is Sahiba Didi now?'

I looked at the full moon beautifully perched against the charcoal sky. A few bright stars twinkled around it. Their radiance matched that of Akshara's face. It was the first time I had seen her so happy and excited.

'Fantastic,' I replied. 'She is very happy. She can see Siddharth, talk to him and laugh with him. Both of them are very happy. And . . . and, just like she said, she continues her good deeds.'

'Wow, Harry! Does that mean Mummy would also return if I do a thousand good deeds?'

'Yes, sure.'

'Okay then.' She got down from the bench and looked me in the eyes. 'From tomorrow onwards, I'll also start doing good deeds. I'll do a thousand of them quickly and get my mummy back!'

'That's great, Akshara.'

Behind her, the park wore a deserted look. People continued trickling out after their evening routine of jogging and exercise. The ones left in the park sat on the benches and were engaged in a playful banter. Every now and then, a chuckle would break out, echoing in the entire park, and then fade out in surprising regularity.

It was getting close to eight. 'Don't you have to go, Akshara?'

She waved a casual hand. 'Later. I'm just thinking how I would do my good deeds. Would you also help me like you helped Sahiba Didi?'

'Okay,' I said. 'Sure.' It felt good to see a wide smile on her face. I'm sure she was smiling like that after a long time. 'So you liked the story?'

'Oh I loved it, Harry! Just like you said.'

'I also said that the story would help you. So did it?'

'Of course, it did. It'll help me bring my mummy back. That'd be great. I'll be so happy . . . so happy . . .'

She suddenly stopped talking and slowly sat back on the bench. Her expression grew grim. 'Oh my God . . . was I . . . was I imagining all of this?'

'What do you mean?'

A minute later, she turned to me. She blinked her eyes a few times. 'You don't exist, Harry, do you?'

'What nonsense?' I said. 'Of course, I exist.'

'No, you don't . . . you don't. Daddy was right. Doctor Aunty was right. I imagine things. That is why they give me these medicines. I imagined you telling me this story but all this while it was actually me.'

'And why would you think so?'

'Because . . . because . . .' she trailed off and big, salty tears emerged from her eyes. She blinked and wiped them off. 'I think I wanted to reinforce the thought that Mummy would return and become my guardian angel. I . . . I made this entire story up to convince myself that. Don't you see, Harry . . . oh wait, I'm doing this again. Why am I talking to you?' She tore her gaze away from me and looked up at the sky. 'I created Harry. He's nothing but a figment of my imagination.'

'I'm not a figment of your imagination, Akshara! I'm real. This story is real. I really helped Sahiba. Siddharth did return as her guardian angel.'

'No, no!' she pressed her ears. 'I knew every element of the story right from the beginning. I knew about guardian angels from a fantasy book I read. Mummy told me about Yama and Chitragupta. I read in a short story blog that a thousand good deeds can make a miracle. Oh God, all this while I had been narrating the story to myself!'

'Akshara, you're not imagining anything . . .'

'Oh no!' she exclaimed, thumping her forehead with her right hand. 'I even created the characters of the story from my real life. Ginny is Mishi. Yes, she's exactly like her. Sidhu Uncle is Mummy. Both of them are dead and used to always help people, and . . . and I'm Sahiba! Even the dog in the story and mine are the same!'

'Akshara . . . Akshara . . .'

'I made this whole thing up.'

'Akshara!' I screamed.

She looked at me and surveyed me from top to bottom.

'I exist, Akshara,' I said. 'You did not imagine anything. Why do you think I came up to you in the first place? I told you, right, that I can hear the sufferings of the people around me? It's a gift from Yama. That's how I helped Sahiba. And that's how I heard you from a distance the day we met. So I walked up to you to help you.'

She shook her head. 'No, no, all that is just a story I cooked up.'

'Akshara, I told you those psychiatrists think they know everything. They do not. You really can see me. And that's because I exist. Don't let them play with your mind.'

She continued shaking her head. 'You're lying. You're just a voice in my head. And I don't hear Mummy's voice either.' More tears came out. 'I imagine that. Doctor Aunty is right.' She lowered her head and continued sobbing. She must be thinking that she lost her mummy again.

'No, Akshara, she's not.' I said. 'Doctor Aunty is not right. You remember I asked once if you were a believer or a cynic? You said you were a believer. So believe me. Please.'

Slowly, she turned to look at me, her wet eyes and moist cheeks reminding me of Sahiba. 'Really?'

'Yes, Akshara. Really. If you are a believer, you will believe that these things do happen in real life. You will believe that I exist. Sahiba exists. Yama exists. You will believe that Sahiba did a thousand good deeds. That God did appear and make Siddharth her guardian angel.'

She stared at me, her two beautiful eyes lost in confusion.

'And if you are a cynic, like so many out there, then of course you'd think that I'm just a figment of your imagination and that you imagined the entire story. Decide which one you are.'

Before she could answer, a shrill voice from our right cut in. 'And there you are!'

It was Shilpi Aunty. She was panting and looked worried. 'I've been looking everywhere for you.'

Akshara swallowed nervously. 'I . . . I . . .'

'Why did you lie to me about being at Mishi's place? And have you been sitting here all evening by yourself?'

'No, I was . . . ' She turned to me, shook her head and then looked at Shilpi Aunty, 'I was just . . .'

Shilpi Aunty frowned. 'Are you imagining someone again? You know how much your father hates it when you do that.' She offered Akshara a hand. 'Come, let's go home. You haven't even eaten anything since afternoon.'

Akshara hesitated, then took her hand and got down from the bench. Slowly, they began walking away from me. Just when I thought she wouldn't, Akshara glanced behind her shoulder. She looked at me one last time impassively, before turning back.

Few moments later, she let go off her hand with a sharp jerk from Shilpi Aunty's grip and started running towards me.

'You want to believe me, don't you, Akshara?' I asked her.

'I want to,' she said. 'But I don't know if I should.'

'Don't be a cynic, Akshara. There are so many out there.'

'I don't know, Harry,' she replied. 'I . . . I still don't know if you are real.' She began retreating slowly. 'Goodbye.'

'I'll leave that decision to you then,' I said. 'Goodbye, Akshara. It was very nice meeting you.'

'Goodbye, Harry.'

'Goodbye.'

Author's Note

When my grandmother passed away a few years ago, I was shattered. She was perfectly fine one instant, and the next, she was gone. It made me think about life and death a lot those days.

She was a deeply religious woman, and the faith and belief I have in God today, I attribute much of it to her. She'd talk a lot about heaven and hell, and the repercussions of our deeds in the afterlife. Honestly, I never paid much heed to it. There are enough problems in this life, and I'd rather not be worrying about the next one now.

One day, out of the blue, not long after my grandmother's death, an idea crept into my mind (as is always the case with ideas). It was about a girl left devastated by her mother's death. I began to think a lot about her. What happened to her mother? And then it got me thinking about my grandmother, heaven and hell, and what became of her.

This became the foundation of my story. Everything in the book is, of course, fiction and a result of, what I would like to believe, my hyperactive imagination.

I really hope you enjoyed reading the book.

Lastly, in case you want to know, I'm a believer and I sincerely believe in Harry and his story. I hope you do, too.

Acknowledgements

To my entire family, for their unconditional love and support.

To M and A, for listening to the story at its nascent stage, for believing in it and for constantly assuring me that it is a good one whenever I used to fret writing it.

To the entire team at Penguin Random House, especially Gurveen and Milee, for having faith in my storytelling ability, and to Shruti, for all her efforts.

To my constant readers, for their support and love, with a special mention to Mitali Parmar, Shebby Tasnim, Juhi Salim, Shelo Aura, Harini Ganesh and Mohammed Danish.

Thank you all.